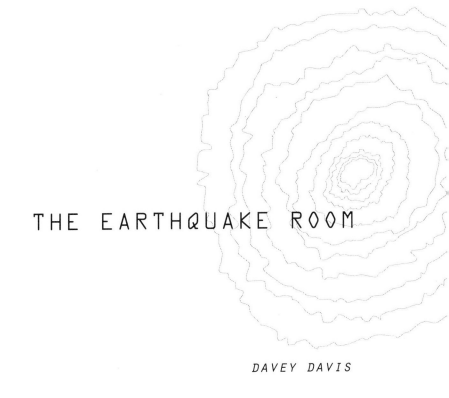

THE EARTHQUAKE ROOM

DAVEY DAVIS

© 2017 TigerBee Press and Davey Davis

ISBN 978-0-9970444-7-8

Cover art by Kitty Davies
Book design by SamDakota

Printed in the United States of America

For more information visit
www.tigerbeepress.com

THE EARTHQUAKE ROOM

DAVEY DAVIS

TigerBee Press

When you're expecting bad news you have to be prepared for it a long time ahead so that when the telegram comes you can already pronounce the syllables in your mouth before opening it.

[Robert Pinget]

THE SORE

it opens like a mouth: cornerless, with a slight perforation at its center. but in every other way, it's unlike a mouth: swollen and spherical, too circular to resemble lips, its redness crowding pale strips of skin that split open to reveal a waxy, sickly whiteness.

k thinks it looks kind of like an asshole, a very tiny one, an enflamed and glimmering replica of the one—bea's—under which it appeared only last night.

oh man, k says.

is it? asks bea.

shit, says k.

is it? asks bea again.

i think it is, says k.

are you sure?

do you want me to take a picture so you can see? asks k.

they bend over the phone together while k expands the image with her fingers. bea is sitting up now, holding her panties in her hand.

i think it is. k's thumb twists under her teeth. *i'm so sorry, bea.*

bea looks away from the phone. *it's okay*, she says. she sighs. bea doesn't think it looks like an asshole. her first thought was *barnacle*.

k begins to pace the strip of hardwood at the foot of the bed, thumb still going, her other hand running through her hair. *i don't even know how i gave it to you there*, she says. *i haven't had one for months.*

i know, says bea.

the last time was when we were in Mendocino and that was in March. remember?

i know, says bea.

you know i'd never do anything to you if i thought i was going to have one. if i had a feeling i was going to get one.

i know! says bea. *really, it's okay.*

it's not okay. k knows she is talking too much, but she's afraid that if she stops, she will cry.

it was probably going to happen anyway, says bea, which is correct. as usual, she is being rational.

i'm so selfish, k says, halting in her circuit. she glares out the window. *how the fuck did this happen?* she sits down, throws her head into her hands, hunches her shoulders over her knees.

as a child, k had often been dramatic. when she was upset— ignored by the boys, in anguish over a dead cat in a storm drain—she would weep and turn red and hurl her body to the ground. a few times, she was sent home by her teachers, who feared the school would be held liable if she hurt herself.

as an adult, k is rarely so expressive, which is something she secretly prides herself on. over the years, she has mastered expressionlessness, a measured and relentless restraint. only those who are very close to her, and there aren't many, witness anything as obvious as tears. this is why, when she allows herself to show her feelings, or rather, when her feelings break free (a brace of frenzied dogs), more escapes her than she knew she could even contain.

bea pulls her panties back on. *don't worry so much*, she says. *it's not a big deal*. even though she believes it to be true, bea speaks softly, with trepidation. she is keenly aware of martyrdom, which she has always found difficult to avoid. like all martyrs, bea finds it easier to endure than to compromise.

even so, she scoots closer to k and puts her arm around k's waist before, quickly, moving it up around her shoulders. she smooths k's hair with the palm of her hand, going fast to communicate authenticity. *it's fine*, she says. *it's really okay*. she shifts her weight against k's body, trying to ignore the itching. if she were alone, she would look at the photo again, at her sores—or rather, the one sore and its constellation of rosy little florets that range from the lowest point of her anus down her perineum like a red-hot tail.

it isn't your fault, bea says. *it's nobody's fault. and anyway, it's not a big deal.* and it doesn't feel like a big deal to her. why should it bother her? they're just some sores.

k manages to press the tears back down into her throat. the core of her aches, but at least the threat of crying is gone. still, she needs to know. *if it isn't my fault, then whose is it?* her question leaves an empty space, summoning ghosts (the past bodies of bea, and all the bodies that have known them).

bea doesn't know what else to say, so she continues to do, embracing k's self-embrace. k knows this is supposed to be reassuring, but she doesn't feel reassured. she feels caged, like a dead bug trapped in its own mortified legs. the feeling intensifies as bea gently pries up k's head and kisses the inner corner of each of her eyes, the places where k's sadness populates, where her skin creases, moves, threatens to overflow.

furrowing her forehead, k feels yet another thing: a love for bea as active as a wish, which makes her feel like this: she wants desperately to be alone.

THE BIG ONE

as she used to write on her dating profiles, bea enjoys her alone time; popular people have this luxury. on the infrequent evenings when k is hanging out with Glory, and Claire and bea's other friends are unavailable, and she has no political meeting, class, or other event in her calendar, bea makes the most of her solitude.

tonight is no different. first, for her big, extravagant plans: she will give herself a facial and a pedicure, beginning with the facial so she can scrub her bedroom floor and dust the furniture while the clay sets, and maybe throw a load of laundry into the machine on the first floor. then, when the chores are done and her face is rinsed, she'll start on her toes, but not before assembling everything she'll need on the nightstand by her bed: a mondo mug of ginger tea, a fresh joint, lotions for all the different kinds of skin on her body, her laptop, and her sewing kit, because after she does her toenails, she has a few patches to add to her jacket (#BLM; No Face from *Spirited Away*).

when everything is ready, bea opens her laptop, settles herself against her pillows, and lights the joint. the cat is curled on the throw at the bottom of the bed, purring like a machine. it's when she's making a few last-minute changes to her playlist—deleting this (Willie and Marlon) and adding that (Nina and Dolly)—that she notices a tab she left open earlier in the afternoon. she hesitates, and then she clicks on it. by the time she finally looks up again, the music still hasn't been started, the joint is consumed, and the cat is long gone.

it's been like this lately. somehow, one YouTube video multiplies into a browserful, two minutes of running time unspooling into hours. with increasing speed, bea darts from tab to tab, sinking into the footage (AMAZING EARTHQUAKE IN TAIWAN! TOP 10 EARTHQUAKE IN WORLD!), quickly losing track of everything she's trying to watch: water slopping out of swimming pools; houses tumbling down hillsides; men and women vaulting piles of fallen boxes mere inches ahead of ceilings collapsing; children clinging desperately to nearby adults, still under the impression that they can be protected. bea keeps moving, skipping ads and cultivating a chain of buffering videos, the screens arranging themselves (concentric Hydra heads) in an array of panicked faces, cackling alarms, crumbling edifice.

many of these videos begin seconds, even minutes, before the earthquake does. as a narrative device, establishing normalcy (a world to be ended) is great for building tension, but as a result bea has spent hours watching what, without the certainty of doom, would have otherwise been boring: people walking to work in Paracas, a Bangladeshi taxi frozen in a traffic jam, a black-and-white woman fumbling through her purse for change. they have become interesting because bea knows that they are endangered, that at some point soon they will be running for their lives, or even suddenly, violently dead—crushed, stampeded, burned, drowned. (is that what fascinates her? that earthquakes are every nightmare in one act of god?)

but she can't just wait for that moment to happen—she has to know beforehand when it will be. at the beginning of each new video, she skips ahead, hunting for the exact moment of inevitable. only then can she go back and watch it from the beginning. of all her hours of earthquake footage, most have been spent in this pre-earthquake reality, adding up to an exponentially longer period of time than the disasters themselves. bea doesn't know this, any more than she knows why she feels compelled to watch in the first place. what does it mean to zero in on surveillance footage of one person, a stranger—an old woman in Kathmandu, a little boy in Wellington—and wait for them to die? what is it about the moving red line at the bottom of the video, a poppy-scarlet lurid as the sand in the Wicked Witch's hourglass, that makes her fear worthwhile?

it is a little after midnight when bea gets up again. on the toilet, she raises her arms, shoulders stiff from hunching over her screen for so long, to sniff the bitterness beneath them. when she returns to her room, she sees that her patches, unmoored, have fallen to the floor. the cat is still gone, and her toenails are still the same color they were when she was born. approaching from behind the screen, where she can't see it, she closes the laptop and sets it on her desk.

blearily high, bea goes to bed in the sense that she is located in her bed, under the covers and lying prone, but she doesn't fall asleep. she should be upset—her evening did not go as planned, and bea's love of order and consistency is a long-running joke among her friends—but she isn't sure how she feels. she makes noises with her mouth, but the cat fails to appear. in the silence (her roommates, a student and a dog walker, are early risers; lights out hours ago), her phone shudders on the nightstand. it's a text from k.

hi baby. falling asleep. what u do tonight?

it's a simple question that bea can't come up with an answer to. for several minutes, she looks at the screen, her thumbs poised over its light. there is no reason to lie, except that she wants to. but why? bea believes in honesty, makes a point of practicing it as radical axe-grinding in a world in which women are trained to disguise all things that are inconvenient to patriarchy, including their truths. but she is high, and tired, and, for reasons she doesn't understand, embarrassed by the hobby that has recently become a habit. when she responds, her fingers move woodenly: **not much. watched a movie.**

k's reply comes tailed by a bloodred heart. **sounds fun bb.**

INSOMNIA

k keeps a glass of water by her bed and never lets it go dry, getting up to urinate four, five, six times a night. she sits on the toilet in the dark long after her bladder has emptied, flicking through her phone (POTUS BLAMES "ILLEGAL IMMIGRANTS" FOR CLIMATE CHANGE), accumulating headlines. sometimes she texts Glory, but Glory, who has to be at the café by 6 a.m. most mornings, is usually asleep hours before k needs her the most.

when she can no longer stand to be in bed, stretched out like a starfish, toes pointed through the sheets toward the ceiling, k gets down on the floor. she lies on the carpet under the open window, her head propped against the wall, and waits for the next accident, listening to the noises from the street: sourceless screams, car alarms. or she counts (*one Mississippi, two Mississi-*) the seconds between tremors, so faint she only knows they are happening by the ticking of the blinds. *i'm taking those bitches down*, says Glory whenever a tremor rattles through her second-floor apartment, the blinds clattering (a handful of marbles thrown at the wall). but she's been saying that for years, and they're still up.

when an accident finally happens, k gets to her knees and pulls the blinds apart to watch the aftermath. she bets on whether the maintenance team (they always arrive before the ambulance) will have removed all traces—exploded garbage cans, twisted fenders, burning tires—before sunrise.

insomnia is easier at her apartment, when she's alone. if she stays the night with bea—and on their nights together, they almost always sleep at bea's place—k has to hide it. most of the time she manages to stay in bed with bea until morning. the first few hours are alright, but after 2 a.m., after she's gotten sick of whatever book she brought with her and turned off her phone, desperate to escape its information (STATE'S PREMIER SEISMOLOGIST MOVED EAST THREE MONTHS AGO, SOURCE REVEALS), there's no way to make the time go faster.

the dark moves in waves around bea's bedroom, obscuring the dresser and its pyramid of gems, the homemade cat tower, the bromeliad in its fat, pebbled ceramic, before revealing them again a few moments later. when the shifting gloom allows, k examines each individual object as well as she can, though by now she's bored by every surface, plane, and corner. she forces herself to do this for as long as she can stand it. only when she has exhausted the room's distractions, or when she is weak and can't control herself, does k turn to bea's body.

it is a bad idea, k knows, to linger over the source of her insomnia, but she is often weak (if thinking about bea hurts her, does that mean she can't love her?). she holds the inside of herself ramrod straight, trying to remember what bea's body was like the night they met, as if it were a metric for quantifying guilt. throbbing like an undersea flower, she vacillates between loving bea, who curls around k—her breath warm on her shoulder, recharging the heart that burns to help people—and wishing they had never met.

k remembers a show they went to in Berkeley last year. a pit had boiled into being and bea had joined in, ferociously happy. as k watched from the side, a large man—his eyes concealed by dark-tinted spectacles, his yellow hair at a 2 on the clippers, his knuckles stained with eights—wheeled into bea, knocking her to the ground. k watched his jackbooted feet collide with bea's ribs as he stumbled over her body, her face stretching open in shock, her lower lip almost inverted.

k raced to her, shoving past the man and other men, reaching for bea's hand, but the man had lost his balance again and somehow couldn't (wouldn't?) move out of her way. k remembers fearing for bea and bea's body, her fingers reaching toward nothing. k can't remember if she pulled bea up herself, or if she eventually was able to get up on her own.

other than a few bruises, bea had been alright. but a lifetime of bruises, of men unaware of their own shapes, of street harassers and queer bashers and shitty dads and boyfriends and bosses—how could bea have escaped unscathed? (the answer: she couldn't. she hadn't.) even in the safety of bea's bedroom, a place where the tremors somehow seem to happen less frequently, alone together in the darkness, k is afraid for bea, and her body, and of the ways her own body will inevitably fail it, has already done permanent damage. (*please just ignore him*, said Glory, her hair coiled like a hundred sacred serpents, as she walked a little faster and a little closer to k. *i don't have the energy for that shit today*.

eventually, the crowd benignly devoured the man and his slurs behind them.)

k remembers a party at Ken's house. someone strung up the words *queer love is healing* on his bedroom wall in a font that was pink and glittery and beautifully faggy. everyone danced and fucked and got high all night, awakening the next morning in scattered piles of soft skin and sour breath, the imprints of heels, corsets, fingers, binders, floggers, lipstick deep in their flesh. a few years later, Ken still hasn't taken those words down.

queer love is healing. k does not always feel like her love heals. sometimes she feels like it damages, curtails, deadens and dead-ends. now that she has hurt bea, how is she any better than the men that preceded her? how is her body, and its repercussions, any different from theirs?

one of k's strengths is her ability to convince herself. she wants to believe the things that hurt bea hurt her, too (she loves her, and what else is love?), and so she does believe it: if her mouth infected bea's body (boba gleaming in an empty cup), then she has also reinfected herself: herpes squared, again and then again, a row of sores growing into a grid, a wall, a pyramid, an eternity.

but it is not within k's power to heal bea, no matter how much she wants to. guilt is no cure, though k's has a relentless, if faulty, logic: the things that hurt bea must hurt k, but the things that hurt k may hurt only k. (*if my pain is greater than yours, then perhaps the pain i caused you isn't so bad. perhaps i am forgivable.*)

all of this rationalizing is based on a premise even flimsier than that of her original guilt, which is this: that bea wants k to suffer as punishment for infecting her, and that k's guilt is not enough, not satisfactory, although it would have been, had bea actually wanted it, which, of course, she does not.

bea sleeps on, leaving k to her logic, a lonely mythology that insists, with unrelenting brutality, that suffering can be atoned for only through more suffering. k finally breaks down and turns on her phone again. mercifully, it will soon be time to go back to work.

THE SORE

on the nightstand in bea's bedroom, next to the candles and the lotions and the lamp, is a bottle with her full name and medical number printed across it. it pops open easily and she pours a single pill into her palm. she swallows it dry, a skill learned from her years of taking vitamin supplements.

bea wants to reach into her underwear and run her fingers over the sore and its constellation (a field of bleached stones), but she doesn't. when her doctor emailed to confirm her test had come back positive (*HSV-1 ... recommend not having sexual contact until ...*), she had allowed herself exactly one evening to cry alone in her bed. in between checking her phone for texts from k that she forced herself to leave without reply, she had reached to feel herself there, pressing down even though it hurt.

since then, she hasn't touched it—unless it is with gloved fingers, to apply the ointment her doctor prescribed for the pain—nor has she cried. the world has already moved on, generating new tragedies, new moments of humiliation and weakness (NO CHARGES FOR OFFICERS WHO FIRED INTO CROWD OF PROTESTERS). this one, having by now eclipsed the peak of its inflammation (jaundiced, unjust), is already almost gone.

bea replaces the bottle on the nightstand and smooths the bedspread with a careful palm. there are much worse things, really, than some harmless little sores.

SWITCHING

neither remembers the first time very well, because of course they were both drunk. most of what happened has gone missing over the length of their first year together, but both have in their possession a few fragments from it, some that the other wouldn't even recognize.

most of these moments aren't even real memories. they're more like ingrained sensations (the cold wooden floor; a dripping hand) that anyone with an imagination could make up for themselves. bea's include a certain string of kisses, significant because there hadn't been many kisses that night overall. she doesn't know why this is, though this doesn't mean she's troubled by it, and neither does k, although this is the sort of thing it would be in her character to worry about, if she remembered. k tends to worry about a lot of things. bea worries, too, but differently. *usefully*, as k says.

it doesn't matter that they were too fucked up to remember the first time, because they know it was good. so was the second time. it was the third, or fourth, or fifth time—an early time, a time before they were really together, when what they were doing could still have been called casual— that it happened:

bea on her back, knees pulled up under her chin like a collar, her arm around k's neck, k's warm, hard hand fucking her. when bea came, she pulled k closer, put her other arm around her; as she re-emerged, she did not wonder, as she had the first or second time, if this might be too intimate, too much too soon. otherwise, this time had started out like the times before: k fucking bea with her hand, her skin slicked with dark, velvety blood. (BAD CREDIT? UNDER 30? HEALTHY PLASMA DONORS GET REDUCED INTEREST RATES ON STUDENT LOAN DEBT!)

but the third, or fourth, or even fifth time was different, because it was the first time that k asked bea to do it to her.

yes, bea said, *of course*. but she was ashamed. it had never even occurred to her to offer to do it this way. why not? she reminded herself of the first time she went down on another girl, of how nervous she had been, but that it had been okay. this made her feel better, but then k brought out the device from a plastic box stored beneath the bed, and her shame returned.

you know, i haven't really topped a lot before, bea admitted, taking the cock from k's hands. this was almost true. she had actually never topped anyone before, not like this. she told k this now because she believes in honesty, and while it wasn't their first time together, it was still only the third, or fourth, or perhaps the fifth time. she was older than k, but had quickly understood that she was less experienced; she did not think k knew this. unlike k, bea had been straight for many years before she came out. before she moved to

Oakland, none of the queers she had been with had ever expected to do this sort of thing.

oh, said k. *i thought you said you were a switch*. her voice as was soft as an apology. she had been lying back in her underwear, relaxed, but now she shifted, pulling her legs closed.

i mean, it's fine. i totally can, insisted bea. she couldn't deny that "switch" had appeared in her profile, somewhere. had it been true, or just wishful thinking? when she was masturbating, she thought about fucking other people a lot. was *wanting to fuck* the same as *being the one who fucks*? weighing the cock, she regretted ever thinking the word could be hers. she had, after all, always been *the one who was fucked*.

i just, you know ... bea fought to say the right thing. *i'm just used to the other way*.

oh, said k.

k's parents had not wanted children but made several of them anyway, of which k was the youngest by almost six years. as a result, she had the experience of being the youngest but of also being an only child, one who spent a great deal of time alone. on k's left bicep is a tattoo of a flaming red heart. inside the heart it says, in a large and furious script, *Mom*.

well, k said, *you don't have to do it, of course*.

bea wanted to do it but she was afraid, and she forgot her belief in honesty: to conceal her embarrassment, she laughed. she brayed. it was so loud and awful—flush up the walls, scoring the ceiling and blaring back on the bed (a movie demon unleashed from a haunted relic)—that in that moment bea hoped she would never laugh again.

now, more than a year later, bea remembers trying to pretend the laugh hadn't befallen her. she remembers pulling the straps up around her thighs, focusing on them so she didn't have to look at k's face (she does not know if k remembers this). she remembers adjusting the straps too quickly, so the harness was tight around her waist but loose everywhere else, the cock drooping, an un-erect tumescence. she remembers slowly pulling herself up between k's legs (the first time she mounted a horse, at a barn in Folsom: her foot slipped and she fell on her ass, the dust billowing around her), but she lost her balance, she lumbered and the cock wavered, in ridiculous parody of itself and in gross contrast against the softness of her thighs.

bea caught herself with her left hand but knocked k's legs with her knee. she looked up again, desperately grinning, but k wasn't smiling back. she allowed bea to pull her legs open, lifting up her hips a little, but then, as if on second thought, she wrenched them away and lowered herself back down onto the bed. her mouth was hard, like the bones in her hand.

i think i want to stop, k said.

oh, said bea. *okay. that's okay.* she remembers pulling away. (in k's memory, she recoiled.)

i don't want to make you do anything you don't want to, said k, who had never ridden a horse, but had been in dozens of bike crashes.

of course i want to, of course! said bea. she was kneeling, helpless, the cock jutting out before her, her shoulders slumped like an unwatered plant. *of course! i'm sorry. did i do something? i'm sorry!* she swiftly flipped onto her back, struggling to pull off the harness so she could take k in her arms.

i think i just want to go to sleep, k said. she rolled over and away from bea. her shoulders collapsed inward, her body shrinking. bea remembers staying in her own cold corner of k's bed until the next morning. k recalls sleeping alone.

this happened on their third, or fourth, or fifth time together, and it happened other times, too. variations of it, whatever it was, continued well into their knowing each other and deep into their love, and when it happened—when bea was not gentle, or k was not ready; when bea was insecure, or k was angry—the air would get thick, premonitory, predatory, and sex stopped being sex and became something else. sometimes, when this happened, one or the other of them would have this thought: *we're going to break up, aren't we?*

but neither of them ever said it, afraid that words would make it so.

A PROPOSAL

i think you should do it to me, k says.

hm? bea is watching the Seismic Update. a long splinter, hazardous to her lips and gums, has almost halved one of her chopsticks, but she doesn't feel like getting up to piece together a new set from the boneyard in the kitchen drawer. eyes glued to the laptop, she takes another bite.

give it to me, k says.

give what? asks bea. still chewing, she looks up from the screen.

give it to me in the same place, says k. she gestures vaguely downward and behind herself, arm winging in a single motion. *the next time you get one on your mouth.*

in the silence, the Update buffers. below the mountain of gallon containers on the screen: GOOD CREDIT SCORE? GET DISCOUNTED BULK WATER RATES UPON APPROVAL!

oh Jesus, says bea. her mouth is still full, the food almost spilling out (a mockery of a drowning person).

k's idea isn't complicated, but she's never been good at making herself understood. *so it would go like this, right?* she begins. she forces herself to speak slowly. *the next time you get one, we could use like a swab or something, and transfer it to me, and then i'll get one there, too. and then we'll both have it in the same place.* she's moving her hands like she's pitching something in a meeting, though k has never worked in an office before. *i mean, think about it.*

bea is still trying to swallow her mouthful of noodle and soy.

it would kind of make things fair, you know? k goes on. this is why she did not suggest transferring a sore from her own mouth to her own cunt; the point is parity, not practicality.

bea tries to swallow again, her fist against her chest, but her throat is constricting, her stomach has dropped. she is almost as infuriated by k's proposal as she is by how ridiculous she must look. water springs to her eyes—she thinks she might choke—and then her throat expands just enough to get the food past her gullet.

stop it! she gasps. coughing, she points the fractured chopstick at k, a spot on her chin glistening, her fist still against her chest, and somehow it is still charming. she finally catches her breath. *what the fuck are you talking about?* as a rule, bea avoids arguments she hasn't started, but k's request is so absurd—insulting, even—that she has no choice but to involve herself. intentionally infect k's cunt with herpes? it's the craziest shit she's ever heard.

it's just really been on my mind, says k. she knows it's a stupid idea, but how could the place it comes from—a desire for balance—be wrong? is it stupid to want to fix things? *i just feel so bad about doing that to you,* k goes on. *it would make me feel better if you could do it back to me.*

if bea could know how close k's voice is to breaking, she probably wouldn't jam her chopsticks into the bowl and clank it on the table. she probably would stop being angry. but she doesn't know. no one, not even bea, finds k easy to read.

i can't believe you're serious, bea hisses. *like do you hear what you're saying? i can't believe this.* she shakes her head, turning her eyes back to the monitor. *i can't believe you think i would do something like that.* as if on cue, the Seismic Update suddenly starts again.

k knows that if she tries to argue, she'll cry. she sits down on the couch. she takes one deep breath, and then another.

i already told you, there's nothing you have to make up for, says bea. her eyes are still trained on the screen. *why don't you believe me?*

k doesn't respond. she's busy breathing.

bea lowers her voice; she wants to sound forgiving. *i don't think you understand just how … how wrong that sounds.* she finally looks up at k. she wants this to be over. she wants to move on.

k is getting dizzy. when bea takes her hand, she resists the urge to yank it away. while the Update is wrapping up (TWEET US AT #HOWIPREP FOR YOUR CHANCE TO WIN A YEAR'S WORTH OF WATER-PURIFICATION TABLETS), bea rubs the padded flesh of her thumb.

it's really okay, bea says. *everything is fine.*

GOING ONLINE

k tells herself that no one would ever respond to something this fucked up. but someone will, of course. it's the internet.

a friend of k's had once needed bedbug corpses to convince a skeptical landlord of a very real infestation. the evidence was on her side, but she couldn't find the insects themselves, and her landlord demanded certainty if she was going to pay for fumigation. desperate, k's friend posted a request for bedbug bodies on Craigslist, offering in exchange only the cost of postage.

she got more emails than she could read and was forced to decide on an offer at random. a few days later, there was an envelope in the mail with her name on it. inside was a plastic bag containing twelve desiccated insects and a Post-it note, a pencil-inscribed smiley face dead in its center.

THE SORE

but it's all gone, says bea.

not completely, says k. she's using the flashlight on her phone to see through the afternoon shadows.

well, i can't see anything. i can't feel anything either, says bea. *it's safe.*

there's still some redness, i think, says k. bea feels her edge backward on the bed. over her shoulder, she sees k is looking out the window. she has already told bea that she doesn't want to have sex until bea is completely healed.

weren't you just asking me to give it to you last week? bea snaps. the light undulates, the room stiffens. her own unfairness shocks her.

maybe i should just go home, says k. the bars on the window split her face into pieces.

bea has never been the sort of person to cry about sex. before she came out, she never thought it could be all that important. when she dated men, sex was something she could take or leave. regular or rare, it was always perfunctory, just some time spent, like masturbating or online shopping. she is not a hornier person now that she is gay, just more emotional.

but now bea is crying, because even though she is sitting on her bed naked, k doesn't want to fuck (her). she feels like a baby, naked and crying, wanting what she can't have.

wait a minute, says bea. *you can't just leave! listen.* she curls around toward k, imploring with her hands, water on her face. *it just, it makes me feel like something is wrong with me.* she perches (glued; a burnt egg) on the edge of the mattress, perspiring, although she is naked and the room is cool. *and i'm not lying. it's been gone for two weeks.*

i'm sorry, says k, shaking her head. her tee shirt, the same color as her socks, says, "I SURVIVED LOMA PRIETA '95!"

can't you just tell me what's wrong? asks bea.

the sore isn't gone yet, that's what's wrong! says k. *why are you pressuring me?*

it feels like you don't want to be to close me.

we're close in lots of ways! just because i'm not in the mood right now doesn't mean we aren't.

so is it that you're not in the mood, or is it something else?

Jesus. k's voice is flat, the wrong tone for invoking a long-dead god.

then what is it?

i'm sorry, says k. k speaks less than most people, but she apologizes more. a penchant for apology is something she and bea have in common. *there's nothing wrong with you. i just don't like thinking about what i did. and when i see it—*

but you didn't do anything! says bea. bea talks more than k, and interrupts more than most people, especially when she's upset.

god, i wish you would just listen to me for a second! says k. *this isn't about sex!*

when bea was sixteen, her dad informed her that the divorce was her mom's fault. he left, he said, because of her affairs with other men: neighbors, her boss, strangers she met from the classifieds in the paper. bea waited years to ask her mom about this. when she eventually did, neither of them had spoken to bea's dad in a long time.

ha! said Mom. *he would say that!*

so it's not true?

shaking her head in time with the windshield wipers, Mom surveyed the freeway (WHERE'S THE BIRTH CERTIFICATE? on an ancient sun-baked billboard), more bemused than angry. bea felt she understood her mother almost completely, although there were a few things— small, unshakeable superstitions (she was convinced of the innocence of Timothy McVeigh) and one or two bad habits (gnawing paper)—that occasionally led her to wonder.

if you have to know, i just didn't like sex with him that much, Mom said. *and he knew it. and if i wasn't gonna do it with him, the only way he could feel good about it was to say i was doing it with everybody else.* her hair was parted sharply, her jewelry loose on her body. *and just for the record, i was the one who left him.*

now bea can't find her shirt. it isn't on the bed or on the floor. she stands up to look for it, resisting the urge to cover herself with her hands (she's in her bedroom, the only place in the world where she can be completely and safely naked, and yet here she is, wanting to hide herself). why is k making her feel ashamed about what she wants? this isn't about libido—she can make herself cum whenever she wants—so why does she care so much?

bea wants to believe that relationships are more than sex, that there is more to love than sex (the unpleasant fullness of a grimacing boyfriend), and the desire for it. she wants this very much, but doubt has freighttrained her. is this really all that being in love is: wondering what the other's desire means, and deciphering why it comes and goes, until it's gone forever? of course there is more, or how could she have any meaningful relationship with anyone? bea thinks: *i am in love with her and that's enough.*

but sex does matter, doesn't it, or why are they together? for that matter, why are they monogamous, against every convention and unlike almost everyone they know? *i am in love with her and that's enough.*

gay? her dad had said. the line on his forehead where his baseball cap (Guerrero Roofing) rested during the day neatly divided slabs of white and brown skin like tiramisu. *what do you mean, gay?*

the absence of sex in a romantic partnership does not have any inherent meaning. it is not necessarily bad, or permanent, or significant (a warning; a deathknell). not having sex—because of exhaustion, arguments, menopause— is inevitable, and yet the world will still go on (COULD FRACKING IN CALIFORNIA TRIGGER THE BIG ONE?). bea has only to read a self-help book or feminist thinkpiece to know this.

so why is she so afraid (lesbian bed death; unfuckable; *who hurt you?*)? *i am in love with her and that's enough.*

bea sighs. *it happened*, she says. *nothing i can do will change it. i'll stay on that medication and never have another breakout again. it will be fine. we just have to move on.*

elbows on the windowsill, k's reflected mouth shapes her response: *i have moved on.* in k's voice, anger and sadness sound identical.

that's obviously not true, bea says. preparing for k to argue, bea forces her posture into a straight line, a shape of defiance. but k surprises her. *i'm sorry*, she says, though she doesn't turn around. in the window, k's skin is grey; the plywood of the fence rises up like a series of burnt matches (a dead end).

the surprise brings with it a sudden fury, the kind bea hates to feel. *i don't want you to apologize!* bea becomes angry like crushed fruit: her perspiration, juices; her complexion, hothouse; her facial muscles relax, softening like pulp. *that's not what i need from you right now!*

so you just need to get laid?

that's not fair! bea is saying it when the plastic hangers in the closet start to rattle, a reminder that she was looking for her shirt. k goes to the nightstand and pushes a glass of water away from its edge. behind her, the door taps in its frame.

bea opens the closet, selects a shirt, and slowly pulls it over her shoulders. she pretends that her head will emerge from its collar in a new dimension, one without anger or fear. she must try again to explain herself to k, but she must also vet her words for both for cruelty and for manipulation (honesty).

she turns around and takes another stab at it. *i just feel like there's something that you're not telling me*, she says.

k, still standing by the door, feels herself begin to panic. the urge to escape is almost as strong as the desire to wrap herself into bea. though she doesn't plan to be, she is honest, too. *i hate that i hurt you*, she says. she wants to be outside, away from this room.

for a moment, bea debates with herself, but decides that honesty doesn't have degrees. *this hurts a lot more*, she admits. behind her, the hangers have stopped shaking. the door sits placidly on its hinges.

so no matter what i do, i'm hurting you, says k, throwing up her hands.

bea wants to contradict her (like a therapist: *your feelings are real and valid*), but then, like the martyr she strives not to be, she doesn't.

the day after the sore appeared, bea spent two hours soaking in Epsom salts. it was uncomfortable, but she reminded herself that it could have been so much worse. they were, after all, just some little sores. some people got HIV. some people got pregnant. (*some people are swallowed by the earth.*) a few sores, as bea continues to remind herself (pearly and painful, feeling as big and sensitive as the eyes of some deep-sea creature), is the world's smallest injustice.

k picks up her bag. *i'll see you later*, she says, opening the door. her sneer lingers through the shiver of her keys, the clink of her bike, the bounce of her weight down the stairs.

bea hears a noise from the bed. the text reads: SEISMOLOGICAL ACTIVITY UPDATE: 2.1, 2:37 PM, OAKLAND, CA. FOLLOW LINK FOR MORE INFO. at the link, she learns that the tremor lasted for a duration of six seconds, although she remembers it feeling much longer.

GOING ONLINE

k tries to write it on her laptop first, but that doesn't work. she tries again with a piece of paper and a pen she found in Glory's kitchen drawer, but that doesn't work, either.

going analog, gramps? Glory says. *what're you writing, a poem?*

k finally gets a few lines out on her phone, her bike (collage of stickers on the seatpost that all say GAY) shuddering against the wall of the train car, the glove from her left hand between her teeth:

> *female bugchaser. i want herpes in a certain place and NOTHING else! prefer female but will consider the right guy. no kissing no sex other than what i need to contract. has to b at your place. bring medical rec's proving you're + what i want and neg everything else. no drugs*

during rush hour, it's easy to look over shoulders and watch people on their phones and tablets. you can read romance novels and messages to friends, critique work emails and bathroom selfies, sit in judgment over feeds refreshed and candies crushed. rush hour is over and k's back is against the panel that opens at every stop, but she still holds her phone as close to her face as she can, afraid someone will see.

she reads and rereads the ad, adjusting it with painstaking care. she loves books, but hates to make her own words; Glory, who went to college and writes like an angel, pens k's job applications in exchange for dinner or foot rubs. but k can't risk showing this to Glory, not after bea's reaction, so she takes her time. she knows, with terrifying certainty, that sooner or later she is going to put it online.

if you agree that there is a spectrum between human and (other) animal, then you might also agree that some people become less human and more animal at particular times, such as when they're afraid (a deer in the headlights; a hare in the crosshairs). but k isn't immobilized by fear. she is electrified by it. when she is afraid, she can't stop moving, can't prevent herself from doing. since the sore appeared, she has been trapped in furious action, unable to stop working, pacing, thinking. more hours on her bike has meant a bigger payout, of course, but she would cash that money and put a match to it if she thought it would help her sleep, or stop thinking about what she's done (*bea's body*).

since the sore, she's begun wearing headphones whenever she's on her bike (bea is now unintact, is no longer safely in health, no longer untrammeled and unmarked and empty of k), wondering distantly if she'll eventually go deaf from the noise, like an aging rock star but even more broke. the worst part is the headphones don't even help. she doesn't need to hear her mind to know what it's doing.

THE SORE

eh i'm alright, texts Claire. how's life

good, responds bea. busy.

bea wants to tell Claire about what is happening with her
and k, but she can't bring herself to do it. if she does, she'll
have to write out, letter by letter, the questions she allows
to go unanswered inside her head. is she willing to break up
with someone (with k) because they aren't having sex? and
if not (and she is not, at least not right now), then what *is*
the problem? how can this one kind of physical intimacy—
certainly not the only kind—outweigh everything else?
there are people (which people?) who are in love for decades
without having much sex. some people are in love without
any. bea thinks: *i am in love with her and that's enough.*

yeah haha, texts Claire. you're too busy with your gf to
spend time with me.

not true! feeling defensive, bea follows up this text with
another: an emoji of two little hearts nestling like lovebirds.

i know, i'm teasing. Claire sends her own emojis, brilliant as a string of Christmas lights. i'm just jealous of you guys. jealous that u have each other & jealous that she has u!

Claire is not single, but her only point of reference for romance is the string of shitty dudes that led up to her current dude, the less shitty Nick, who is still (Claire knows, at a level not quite deep enough to be comfortable) pretty shitty. most of her friends are queer, and she has developed the bad habit of idealizing their relationships. *i keep waiting to wake up and realize i'm gay,* she once told bea. *i want to escape from heterosexuality, too.*

bea empathizes, or used to anyway. there was a time when she viewed her own trajectory as a kind of escape. and this made sense, because the intensity of gay attraction and love was like nothing she had ever felt before. what was it that Frank Ocean said when he came out? something about falling from a plane? that's what it felt like to bea, too: a drop from a great height, down to where there was atmosphere, where you could finally, for the first time, breathe. who needs heights? the depths are where life is. the great rifts at the bottom of the ocean where things live, grow, glow, are hidden away only in the sense that those above are unaware of their existence.

but bea has learned that falling in love is different from the work of loving, and that the incredible good luck of being a dyke comes with many of the inconveniences of straightness. there are the same arguments, anger, resentments, of course; but just as the beautiful parts of queer love are magnified, so are its uglinesses. being misunderstood by men felt so normal to bea back when she was straight that it didn't feel particularly important that her male partners didn't understand her, either. but being misunderstood by other women, or by k, feels unbearable, because it is not supposed to be that way. their language is supposed to be identical, their communication perfect.

just as the emotional parts of relationships have become more intense (acute; elemental; gay), bea has come to the alarming conclusion that sex has also taken on that same gravity. she does not like this, does not want to allow sex to have that importance, to become something in which you participate, open-eyed and focused, rather than going off somewhere else, thinking about porn or a far-off beach or a building falling down (collapsing like an accordion in a cloud of dust). sex prompts questions that she'd rather go unasked (*what happened?* said Dad. *why didn't you tell me?* said Mom. *don't you like that?* said Greg). for her own very good reasons, bea wants to believe that relationships are more than sex. she wants this very much.

we're kind of having a fight right now, texts bea. **i guess we're sort of having a rough patch.**

don't worry, girl. everyone has those, responds Claire. she is an excellent friend, one who has perfected the art form of decontextualizing sadness at just the right moment. and bea has to admit that Claire is right. k is not her first partner, this fight not her first fight, this encroaching devastation (her first girlfriend, unknowing, touched her in the wrong place, in the exact wrong way, so bea picked a fight so big that they couldn't not break up afterward) not a unique one in a world of pain.

and they were just some sores! just some little sores that grew because someone, someone that bea loves, touched her, causing a lifetime of occasional, temporary discomfort (OP-ED: AUSTERITY MEASURES ARE WHAT MADE AMERICA GREAT!). what could be as forgettable, as unimportant, as occasional, temporary discomfort, just as normal and inconvenient as a cold? why has this grown so very big?

you're right, texts bea. i'm probably making a big deal out of nothing.

GOING ONLINE

k wants to post a picture along with the ad, but she can't decide what kind. something sexual will get the most attention, but subtlety has its own merits. she examines her face on the postcard-size screen before turning the phone around, pulling it away, watching her body appear.

maybe a strict portrait is better. no angles or filter, just a picture, as direct and honest as a picture could possibly be. (*they're all lies*, announces Ken, closing the cruising app with a sigh of disgust. *what do you care what they look like?* asks Glory. *big dick has no face*.)

k can't show her face, regardless. or maybe she can show it a little bit (distant chin; glance askance; a helpful shadow around the eyes). she can do it without identifying herself, and it might feel more trustworthy, which might draw more replies. if she does that, should she find a wig to wear, so as to appear feminine, and therefore attractive? she knows many people who own wigs, but doesn't think she can borrow one without having to explain.

hustling taught k that when it comes to personal ads, there's a sweet spot on the spectrum of variety and quantity: the number of replies is inversely proportional to their general coherence. the right photo will hit that sweet spot, and once it does, she can get this (fixing; atonement; betrayal) over with. (*bea's body*)

but as she also learned from hustling, there is such a thing as the wrong kind of attention. emails from trolls and wankers won't pay the bills, and they won't get her what she wants now.

k holds her phone out in front of her, turns her head, presses down. it isn't how you hustle, but as whom that makes the difference. she takes another pic, and she examines it, searching for soft angles, analyzing desirability on a scale of porn bots, sponcon, cam girls, dating apps, likes, retweets, Photoshop, male gaze, whiteness, Snapchat, literature, TV, the bodies she finds herself watching as they ascend the stairs up from the belly of BART.

a message dips down the screen. it's from bea. what u doing tonight? come over and sleep w me?

k allows a few minutes to pass before she replies. wish I could. staying late in the city to work.

bea responds immediately. you can come over after. I can leave the key out

k waits for five minutes this time. it's ok. don't want to make u lose sleep. be there tomorrow promise. she added an especially pretty heart emoji before she sent the text.

can bea read the lie? k got off work at the normal time and has been home ever since. she imagines bea in her bed, reading a book, the cat against her knee. k puts this out of her mind. she has other things to think about.

she gets back to work, trying on and then stripping off clothes, yanking them from hangers before throwing them back into the closet, only stopping to glance at, and then delete, the selfies she takes between changes. she pauses once to wait out a tremor (her bed rattles, the photos blur), but then gets back to work, assessing every article of clothing with the eye of a stranger. how many responses will this photo get? or this one, a different photo that is nevertheless identical to the one taken the instant before? what about this one—her face in profile, her torso in a white tank top? will it get at least fifteen in the first twenty-four hours? and what about this one: her thumb pulling a pair of women's underwear only a few centimeters away from an area of her body that, were it visible, would get her post flagged. five? five hundred? how many of the responses will have any sort of potential, sent by a person serious about giving her what she wants?

the trick to finding out what people want is to think like them. anyone who has ever served, cared for, cleaned, or fucked in exchange for money knows this. though she doesn't want to, k finds herself thinking about bea, trying to think like bea. is she still awake? k considers texting her (got off work. can i b your big spoon?), then decides against it, even though she knows bea wouldn't mind, because she loves k, even while she sleeps. imagining this—bea's dreamy lovingness—k feels a surge of shame.

to distract herself, k tries to think like a man; though she specified in her ad that she wants women to respond, she has a feeling, a strong feeling, that this is unlikely. she closes her eyes and then opens them again, imagining them peering out from a skull of maleness, from a mind who might see her request to get infected and become aroused by it.

disgusted, she aims her phone, steadies it, and shoots another selfie.

MONOGAMY

unlike almost everyone they know, k and bea are monogamous. they have been since the beginning.

at first, it was by default. when they met, they fell hard and
fast. bea ghosted her one casual date almost immediately,
and informed a friend she slept with when both happened
to be single that she was no longer available. k didn't have to
do anything because she hadn't been seeing anyone on the
regular.

monogamy was new to k. she was still attracted to other
people, of course, but with bea, she experienced this
attraction without any focus. at the beginning, even when
other people were right in front of her—a precisely styled
femme hanging out at Glory's; a genderqueer line cook
whose bouffant was polished to a bright, anachronistic
patina—she couldn't be distracted. in the months following
bea's entry into her life, no other person had been real,
because they would have had to be visible first.

bea and k decided on monogamy by committee, holding
hands, their feet in cool riverwater, resolving together the

way they would relate and be, an indefinite future with a universe of potential.

you are all that i want, they said to each other.

so gay, k said.

THE NIGHT IT HAPPENED

bea sent k a selfie, her winged eyeliner on display behind a tableau of freshly done fingernails, profile arrayed like a religious icon radiating light, as if from a time preceding perspective, so k could see the masterpiece of her hair— plaited and burning with new colors—falling down her shoulder. she and Claire were getting ready to go dancing.

Claire was in a cosmetology program, though her certification, once she got it, would be a mere formality. a photographer specializing in artists and fetishists and pros, she had been styling hair and fixing homemade manicures for years. then Nick, who didn't mind her work, exactly, but worried about its proximity to the kind of people she worked with, encouraged her to dream bigger.

you could charge more money if you got certified, Nick said, thinking about the Backpage ads he sometimes scrolled through, of the women who leaned over homey beds in their underwear, who used code words and put filters over their faces. *you could work with real clients, not just all those girls you know.*

so Claire went to beauty school. she spent her savings on new equipment and a professional website. she began shooting golden children in autumnal treescapes. she started offering a deal on portraiture, shot in the Headlands or Tilden Park, to bring in affluent new clients. there was good money to be made off techie brides and fifty-year-old white women daring themselves to experiment in Claire's pop-up boudoir.

Claire sometimes didn't know how to feel about these changes, but she liked school because it gave her an excuse to give her friends makeovers. (*who says the world's going to last long enough for you to graduate?* teased bea) that day, she got to bea's early so they could while away the afternoon getting high and practicing their French tips. while they waited for bea's hair to set, they sipped ginger ale from tea cups.

k texted bea back. you so pretty. the heart emoji she sent was crowned with sparkles.

from bea: aw shucks.

from bea again: what are you doing tonight

one foot on the pavement, k was trying to untangle her headphones with her free hand while she waited for the light to change. ken's friend is moving away, she responded. they're having a party for him.

come dance after, ordered bea.

haha. okay I'll try, said k. she would come. she wanted to touch bea's hair with her fingers. she wanted to kiss her face, and the makeup on it.

you don't have to dance. you can stand with me and claire in the corner if the dj sucks, said bea. she knew k didn't like to dance.

k started to text but the light changed before she could read what she wrote. she wanted to pull over, lean her bike against a pole, and write bea a bible of her love, but the app sent in an order—too far away, no time—and anyway, she wasn't good with words (*DUMMY* tattooed on her collarbone).

instead, k sent bea a round face with a heart where its mouth should be, a tarot symbol for the internet age.

ABOUT BEA

there was Greg and there was realizing she wasn't straight. bea doesn't remember which came first, though she does know that both happened during high school. the sequence shouldn't have been important, but it was, because she hadn't meant to be queer any more than she had meant for what happened with Greg to have happened. and if Greg happened first, that meant that he existed before her queerness did. that meant he existed before bea did.

of course i miss her, said bea. *of course i do. it's not something i'm just going to get over.*

i know, honey. i know, said Mom. bea didn't know that Mom had ordered a book, Your Grieving Adolescent, which still hadn't arrived in the mail. *it must be really, really hard to lose such a good friend*, Mom ventured.

she was more than a good friend! bea remembers Mom's misunderstanding, and how angry it made her, and how that anger linked up with the fury she felt knowing that she hadn't talked to Mai when she could have. now it was too late (a photo of Mai tacked to the wall beside her bed in Mom's old apartment, its edges almost white because she'd peeled off the Scotch tape so many times to take it down. looking at it, taking it down, hiding it away, crying again to think of Mai in a box under her bed, in a box under the earth, motionless, before taking it out and taping it back on the wall).

your friends in high school, those girls you bond with, Mom went on, *those are some of the most important friendships you'll ever have. i'm not saying you don't have to be sad—*

you don't get it, spat bea. Mom didn't understand why it was different with Mai, how the devastation of losing a best friend was different, must be different, from the devastation of losing something that could have happened but never would. she suddenly realized, with the assuredness and prescience of teenagers, that it would mark her forever.

could it be that Greg had marked her, too; that he had made her into what she was now? (*what would k think?*) bea couldn't bear this thought, but there it was: the possibility that she had not been born queer, like you were supposed to be, but had been made that way (damaged goods), a side effect of patriarchy, a mistake just like they said. (once, at her dad's church: the pastor said that a girl's purity was like a strand of pearls, and that if she had sex before she got married, it was like giving individual pearls away, one pearl per fuck. with every loss, her necklace was devalued, though the pastor didn't say when her necklace would run out of pearls, or what number of screws would leave her finally a worthless, empty string.)

i know it feels like that, said Mom. *i know it feels like something i wouldn't understand. and i don't, completely. but i've lost people, too, hon, and i know that at some point, you have to dive back into life.*

i just loved her so much, said bea. she didn't want to eat. she didn't want to leave her room or text her friends back. it was easier to hide from the world, back then, when people were slightly less connected and Seismic Updates didn't exist. fresh tears ran hot down her cheeks. *i love her so much.*

had the realization happened before bea said this, or after, when Mom stopped stroking her arm through the bedspread. (before Greg, or after? why can't she remember?) for the first time since she'd sat down on the bed, Mom turned her head, looking directly at bea. for a long moment, she studied her. when she spoke again, her voice had changed slightly. it was still reassuring, the chocolatey warmth of a mother easing distress. but it was also calculating, like she was trying to do long division in her head.

i know it's confusing, said Mom. (the book was supposed to have arrived the day before. *fucking Amazon*.) her arm started moving again. *i know really caring for someone can be confusing at your age. but as you grow up, you realize that a lot of it is just hormones.* she reached over and took a strand of bea's hair between her fingers. *and that's okay. it's a normal part of growing up.*

bea didn't say anything, even though it was then that she knew that how she felt about Mai was the only thing she wasn't confused about. that clarity (a lid fitting into the grooves of its jar)—an exactness, a rightness—was how she knew, and how Mom learned (daddy's little pearl) who she was.

it wasn't until years later that they discussed it again. bea had brought her first girlfriend home, and things seemed to be going well until Mom, nervous, desperate to fill a lull in the conversation, sputtered, *you know, i really had no idea about all this* (gesturing to the space between bea and Cory). *it really just came out of left field for me.*

to cover her tracks, Mom swept them off on a grand tour of her apartment, but it was too late. bea felt the anger welling up inside her, but with the same sense of tidiness that kept her inbox empty and her books in alphabetical order by author, she gathered it up and put it away. Mom had lied about what she did and didn't know, but this was not the first time that she had hidden the truth. it was impossible for bea to be angry about this lie without exhuming the other, and she didn't have the strength to do both.

nor did she have the strength to pretend that the anger felt easy, because she loved Mom and she knew that Mom loved her, loved her so much and so deeply (even though Mom had failed to keep her safe). it hurt to feel anger in the place where that love belonged. when Greg died, bea went home, and Mom hugged her at the door, like she always did, but for the first time, her body felt so heavy, trapped in the bear hug (*Mommy loves you so much; she wants you to be safe*) (but Mommy also let Greg come live with Mom and little bea) (*i still love you mommy*) (even though Greg wasn't allowed around the little cousins) (*i love you baby*) (even though

Mommy has bad memories with Greg, too) (*why can't Mommy see he isn't safe?*), that she couldn't hug Mom back, could hardly summon the energy to hold her body upright in the embrace.

like bea's feelings, the timeline was muddled. cause and effect were obscured, and whatever the sequence, it was undeniably true that what had happened, had happened. it was a confusion bea wished she could just accept (*am i gay because of straightness?*), but she couldn't stand the thought long enough to do it, so she pushed it away, down into the same place she kept her anger when she didn't want it, holding herself in unsteady quarantine.

TROUBLE WITH LOVE

the trouble with instant attraction is that it is, by its very nature, chemical; which is, by definition, volatile; which is, by implication, untrue—if, that is, you are prejudiced against flux and in favor of eternity.

k is suspicious of all her feelings, and in particular the ones that come upon her without warning. no matter how strongly she feels them, her doubt is stronger. for a very long time, she has believed that emotions triggered by sight cannot be trusted. falling in love is a kind of tunnel vision.

this mistrust comes from experience, from years of getting stuck in that tunnel. instant attraction, the way that certain people can evoke a sharp and inexplicable captivation (a lighter flicking), could happen at any moment, and it often did.

the trouble is not the feeling itself. the idea of falling in love, alone and from afar, without ever encountering the object of her desire … every so often, k catches herself thinking that *that* would be the best way to live.

no, the trouble is that the pleasure of this feeling tends to vanish as soon as its object—women and people like k— become available to her. unfair as it is, once that person wants k in return, k doesn't want that person anymore.

my trouble with love, k calls it.

your boring and pathological fear of commitment, Glory calls it. (COUNTING DOWN TO THE BIG ONE? JOIN FUTURBANK AND COUNT YOUR SAVINGS, TOO!)

k's memory is not good enough to keep a tally of all the times her desire has manifested as cruelty. still, a few memories stick around, no matter how much she drinks.

once: a woman in an electronics shop who argued with the man at the counter in Farsi. she played the guitar and loved to knit. a month later, she had blocked or unfriended k on every social-media app.

once: a woman behind a register in thick blue-framed glasses, her heart-shaped face falling open into thoughtless smiles between one customer and the next. her jacket was crowned with a pin that proclaimed both her politics and desires (*I ♥ Being Queer*) all in one slogan. six weeks later, she left a handwritten letter under the welcome mat in from of k's apartment calling k, among other things, a *shitass*.

once: a person in a bodysuit, acrylics, lipstick, and boots— all black—stalking toward k's café table, a moment of divine darkness pierced by the violet script across their tee shirt:

FEMME. when k saw them now, at dance parties and house shows, they looked past k like something vaguely interesting was happening directly behind her.

once: the queer who gave k her first hand-me-down binder. he still wouldn't respond to k's annual texts to meet up at their old café (STUDY SAYS COFFEE WILL BE EXTINCT WITHIN THE NEXT TWENTY YEARS). someone told k he moved to Chicago last year.

once: and again: and many times: through apps, behind desks, under cars, inside food trucks, adjacent to k on their own bikes, a litany, a chorus, a database of reasons why k is no good at loving.

by now, k is old enough to take for granted that desire is unhappiness, but not old enough to resign herself to it. *is this how it's going to be?* she wonders. will it be like this through the rest of her twenties and beyond, until she is old or until she dies or until the world dies, loving immediately but never enough? she wishes she could expect it to someday stop, but there is no reason to think it won't last as long as her body does.

CHANGING

a few weeks before her first anniversary with bea, k began losing control of her body. at the CVS, her hands snatched things—concealer, aspirin, travel floss—she hadn't intended to steal when she entered the store. (QUAKEPREP ASSO-CIATE, said the lapel of the CVS employee who shuffled past. ASK ME ABOUT OUR FIRST-AID TRAINING. YO HABLO ESPAÑOL) she didn't tell anyone about this, not even Glory, who would have understood.

she began losing her strength. the hours on her bike went from challenging to unimaginably hard, and her exhaustion grew heavier than the obligation of rent, always hovering somewhere a hundred years away. she started closing her courier app earlier and earlier in the evening. she did confess this to bea, who dosed her with vitamins, and to Glory, too, who turned up with bunches of glistening dumpstered kale.

but k knew this loss of control couldn't be treated with well-ness because it was not rooted in the body. it came from somewhere else.

though whatever it was still grew inside her, k took what precautions she could against it (a heavy object suspended from burning rope). she began avoiding other queers, attending fewer parties and readings and shows, even when Glory begged her to go. when bea's friends dropped by, she found excuses to hide in bea's room, or just go home.

being alone felt the least precarious. that's why she started to tell bea she was working late when she was actually at home, curled up in a blanket, smoking dried-out nugs she found in the back of her sock drawer. increasingly, it felt like the strongest thing she could do, because now her desire was worse than an attraction that hurt other people: now, if k acted on it *(when),* it would hurt bea.

TROUBLE WITH LOVE

until she met bea, k had always thought of her trouble with love as a flaw.

bullshit, said Glory. *you think being neurotic is cute. like Woody Allen.*

in light of bea, she had reconsidered this stance for the first time in years. perhaps her desire wasn't a flaw but a weakness, a thing that could be controlled through willpower. perhaps the part of her that wanted to be with bea and bea only was one she could nourish, which meant that the parts of her that were afraid to love bea could be starved away.

but how to feed and to starve, respectively? the months passed, and the euphoria of newness faded, as k and bea knew it would. growing in its place was the restlessness k had learned to avoid with distance.

maybe monogamy just isn't for me, said k.

but you don't even commit to multiple people, said Glory. *you don't commit to anyone.*

who says i have to? said k.

nobody, said Glory, *but you want somebody. i know you do.*

i'm committed to you. isn't that enough?

they had spread themselves out flat, the pair of them almost too much people for Glory's little porch. Glory—whose difficulties hardly ever have to do with her partners these days—took a particular interest in k's romantic problems.

it became stronger, this restlessness, even as k's feelings for bea increased. when she woke up next to her, k resisted the urge to touch the downiness of her hairline, the prettiness of her throat, and awaken her before her alarm. she stopped working peak hours, when she made the most money, so they could spend their weekends together. when she was with bea, k experienced a calm she had never felt with another person. being with bea was as safe as being alone, but it was also beautiful.

contrasted with this happiness, k's restlessness, or whatever it was, was all the more frightening. what occasional phenomenon caused her to want to avoid bea, and the long Sunday nights that pushed, too heavily, into the impending work day; the afternoons when all of bea's friends stopped by her place without warning to smoke on bea's couch, at her kitchen table, in the window nook overlooking the neighbor's garden? why did an innocent statement sometimes grow into an argument, and how could the argument, however petty, seem so enormous that k occasionally thought it might be easier to just end it all and disappear and be alone forever? they were happy, so why did k sometimes consider finding a stranger to fuck so she could admit it to bea in a text and then disappear?

ESCAPE FROM HETEROSEXUALITY

when bea answers, Claire is already crying. it's Nick again, of course. over the phone, Claire's voice sounds strange, almost unfamiliar. have they ever done this before? despite the evidence supplied by pre-internet sitcoms, has anyone?

and now he's out somewhere and he won't text me back and he won't call me, says Claire. *he always does this but it still freaks me out. like what if he got hurt or something?*

he's not hurt, says bea. *i'm sure he's just fine.* bea wishes she could kill Nick, but she would never say this to Claire; bea is also a good friend, and her hatred of Nick is not something Claire wants to hear about. but while Claire continues to talk, she becomes distracted comparing their relationships, lining them up next to each other and reckoning all the variables away into two columns: Happy and Sad. she wishes she could return to a time when she believed that simply eliminating men from the equation would mean that all problems could be solved.

i don't think he realizes how much he's hurting me, says Claire. *he wouldn't do it if he knew how much this hurts.*

a memory returns to bea, something that happened last year, shortly after k introduced her to Ken.

i just wish i was a dyke, Ken said. *i hate men.*

you have to stop seeing him, said k. she was rummaging in the freezer for a bag of something frozen. had bea known her better at the time, she would have seen how shaken she was, how angry. *he's fucking insane.*

i know, said Ken, chastened, sinking down into the chair. for a moment, bea could picture him as a little boy, dark-haired and open-faced, thrilled by trains and fireworks and Disney princesses.

but then Ken looked up, and caught bea watching him. suddenly as a power outage, he shifted affects, but not before emitting a vast, shaking sigh. *but don't get it twisted*, he said, lisping hard, raising his voice so k could hear. *boys hitting boys is just queering love, baby.* he laughed, his eyes now rigid as his posture.

shocked, bea felt herself taking a step back. what had she done?

that's a fucked up thing to say, said Glory. she came and stood over Ken, looking down on him. bea had never heard her sound angry before.

you know i'm just kidding, said Ken, rolling his eyes. though he was sitting, he was stepping away, too, getting sucked into the furniture like a horror movie.

bea watched Glory watching Ken, witnessed her eyes jumping, the decision shiver and then, instantaneously coagulate. she feared the worst. but then Glory swooped, collapsing onto the chair and Ken's body, surprising him with a gentle kiss.

i'm sorry he hurt you, Glory said. Ken only resisted for a moment before letting go, nestling into her body, softening into her softness.

TRAPPED

k remembers a conversation with Glory from last fall, not
long after she and bea met.

do you you feel trapped by it? asked Glory.

monogamy? said k. *i don't know. if it keeps feeling this good, it
won't matter.*

and you really have never done it before? Glory marveled over this
piece of information.

nope. bea has. she did for a long time.

so she has practice, said Glory. k remembers the smile in her
voice.

yeah, said k. *but think about it like this: i haven't learned how to do
it right, but i haven't learned how to do it wrong, either.*

k remembers that she didn't feel as confident about
monogamy as she had wanted Glory to believe. even back
then, she had her doubts. she was not afraid to share this

uncertainty with Glory, but she didn't know how to describe it and she feared misunderstanding. it was a complex feeling, to doubt something she wanted so much.

before bea, k had seen monogamy as a set of rules, confining or reassuring depending upon the people living within it. *within*: as if monogamy were a location.

at 3:25 a.m., k watches the light pierce the raindrops (IF GLOBAL TEMP CONTINUES TO RISE, EXPERTS WARN SAN FRANCISCO COULD BE UNDERWATER IN TWENTY YEARS) on the glass. perspective matters, but the degree to which it simplifies, or complicates, is a mystery to her. how is it that she can be so unhappy, but still in love with bea? how is it that the only way she can feel safe is to fantasize about hurting bea, and thus herself, more than she thinks she could survive? each raindrop lands with a crack, like flexing leather.

from the inside looking out, k can see that monogamy is not as she had expected. the place where she and bea now are, the place where they live together—though they have separate apartments in different neighborhoods—is not unlike the warmth of bea's arms, at once a condition and a being and a knowing (the moment in which a need is fully satisfied; a spinal cord, vital and whirring; a bed frame, large enough for two, carved from a living tree).

but k doesn't know if her love is stronger than her weakness. still, up until the night it happened, controlling herself (*ladykiller* tattooed above her right knee) was not a deprivation, like going hungry or staying sober. this is why what happened at the decaying house in East Oakland did not make any sense at all.

THE NIGHT IT HAPPENED

the Woman in Black wanted k first. before everyone got drunk, she had already found her, reaching for her arm without actually touching it.

we're dressed the same, said the Woman in Black, her fingers still extended. k looked down at her body. it was true: black jeans, black-and-blue flannel. both wore a black baseball cap on their head.

but my hair is different than yours, said k. it was not a rebuttal, or even flirtation, but an acknowledgment, a response without intent (a rock dropped down into a crevasse, demonstrating that it is merely a very dark hole). it wasn't as if their outfits were terribly unique in the first place, but that was obviously beside the point.

the Woman in Black grinned. her eyes moved upward from k's boots to the hem of her shirt, then up even further to her throat.

well, she said (perfect canines), *nobody's perfect*.

k heard a voice behind her and seized on it, whirling and escaping, leaving the Woman in Black as far behind her as the walls of the house would allow.

it's a communal QTPOC space. it's a little south of the Lake, went the voice. the person it belonged to was pomped like Prince. around their neck was a little golden watch that didn't tick.

i think i've been there before, Glory said. k positioned herself at her side, trying to give the impression that she had been present for the entire conversation. *it has that trampoline, right?*

earlier that afternoon, Glory had shown up at k's apartment without texting and refused to leave alone. this was why k was here tonight, rather than still at home, although she had been friends with Ken long before Glory ever met him. k nodded agreeably as Glory talked, not daring to look behind her. from nowhere emerged Glory's hand with a coffee mug, and k took a drink of the whiskey inside it.

that's the one, said Prince.

if you ever have a spot open up, you should let me know, said Glory. *my girlfriend and i are trying to find a new place.*

they just met last week, said k, emerging from her almost-empty cup, grateful, for once, for the chance to interrupt. *they're uhauling, big time.*

Glory laughed. *ignore them*, she said to Prince, gesturing at k with a few dismissive fingers. *we've been together for years.*

everyone laughed. k never tried to be funny at parties, but Glory knew how to play along.

though she was always sleeping with someone, by design or by failure, k tended to be solitary. Ken and Glory were friends, good friends, but unlike k, both of them had many other friends. k did not find friendship to be easy. it was easy to gradually fall away from acquaintances, even easier from people who got close.

if i didn't just show up all the time, you'd forget about me, Glory joked, and it was mostly a joke, but it was also a little bit truthful, and k knew it, and Glory knew it, and k loved Glory for loving her anyway, for arriving with food, or weed, or whiskey, or nothing, and letting herself in with her key, and sitting on the couch with k and reading, or getting into bed with her and cuddling, or dragging her outside to go and do something. *before you shrivel up and die in front of your laptop*, Glory would say.

so how do you know Ken? Glory was addressing Prince again.

we met on the-app-that-shall-not-be-named, Prince said, laughing. *it was a long time ago.*

that's how he meets everyone, Glory said. she laughed, too.

he knows every queer in the bay, said Prince.

then how is he always meeting new ones? asked k. alcohol and adrenaline pumping inside her, she was feeling unusually talkative, uncustomarily glib.

because they keep moving here, Glory said. *hey!* she turned around, putting k and Prince behind her, lifting up her voice to match the music. *raise your hand if you were born here!*

in the living room full of queers, no one did, except for Glory, and her, the Woman in Black.

BEA'S BODY

the bedroom is too cold for summer. her weekend of
overtime has ended, but insects still hum inside k's feet. the
bones of her left leg buzz, her hips ache like pregnancy. she
can feel bea's hot, metastasizing body beside her. curled into
a pretty jackknife, her eyes and mouth completely closed,
bea sleeps, as she does everything, perfectly.

it is 2:42 a.m. and k is thinking about the sore. though it
healed weeks ago, it remains in the bed with them, as present
as another person. she sits up for some water. drinking it is
difficult, its flavor distasteful. she is exhausted by her thirst,
but she forces herself to swallow.

k has been watching bea since she fell asleep. her body is
still, but undoubtedly alive. k's own feels like a rotting thing
encased in static—she can't suppress the urge to move, to
fidget (a child at a desk; a guilty dog; a weed growing toward
the light). she tries to expend her energy on motionless
activities—measuring her breath against bea's, listening to
the sound of her own eyelashes on the pillow, tallying up
the miles she put on her bike last week, last month, since
she got her first Schwinn on her ninth birthday—but every

so often she shifts, squirms, shudders anyway. she doesn't understand how bea can possibly sleep through all this (DEATH TOLL CONTINUES TO CLIMB AFTER CHINA'S BIGGEST GARBAGE LANDSLIDE ON RECORD), and yet she does.

k knows that, generally speaking, her body and bea's are quite similar, enough so that there are states to which they'll never move, countries that they'll never visit, queers they will never know because they can't reveal themselves. that is, according to the world, they are *too* much alike to be in love. k used to feel that resemblance, feel the way that her body was the same as bea's, as other bodies: brimful with organs and aswim in blood, in the fluids of vitality and bile, unified by the gristle and bone inside her. she was once biological, like other people, and thereby vulnerable to the same microbes, afflicted by the vicissitudes of temperature and phlegm, caffeine and alcohol, indica and sativa, brunch and broke.

(once, in Bangkok: something like malaria. Glory sat on the bed with her, worrying and tracking her fever, which was intermittent and unreasonable, swelling and bursting beneath her skin by each morning so she could briefly return, exhausted, to real sleep, her skin moist with her sickness and then cold with remission, seeping nightmares all day long until the fever came back at sunset, when the humidity was at its worst. Glory haunted the hostel computer, researching k's nonsense symptoms and emailing with a friend in nursing school.)

it has been three weeks since k has slept more than four consecutive hours, and even that short, fatiguing unconsciousness feels like a physiological taunt. when she slows down long enough for a catnap, she breaks the momentum she needs to keep going to work, so she's stopped making that mistake. but no matter how much she tries to conserve her energy, the hills get steeper, the flats mutate into hills, her thighs scream and her ankles ache, and the sun, glaring off the trolleys, their wires hissing like bats, is too bright, burning her neck, hot and dirty under layers of flannel and Lycra. she has stopped wearing her binder when she rides, and though it's easier to breathe, the exhaustion weighs heavier on her shoulders. her lower back knots like the muscles between her eyes.

sometimes she dozes in the tunnel on the way home, awakening with the last shudder of the train as it ascends again in Oakland, the night black against the blacker cranes. she wants to curl up on the ground inside a train that never stops.

this is not the first time in k's life that her body has refused to sleep. there was last summer, when she got laid off, and two years before that, when Glory was in Texas for six months taking care of her sister during chemo. but even during those times, her body had remained like other bodies: vulnerable to stimuli, excreting waste, generating antibodies: respire, metabolize, repeat: a totality of environment.

something has changed. now her body is different than before. it is no longer churning and cycling in and over itself (a taffy machine hurling and catching viscous pink webs).

now, instead of being biological, instead of being full up of itself with working parts, it has emptied (or filled in; she can't decide which). this k discovered when the sore appeared on bea's body a few months ago.

but how did it happen, and when? k, awake in bed next to sleeping bea, tries to take inventory, feeling her body with her hands. her outside is still the same, misleadingly so. no one, not even bea, can see that something is wrong, that her insides are gone, vanished at the point where they once became visible. where they are meant to be, they just *aren't*.

now k's body is the limit of itself. it is the ring of her nostrils, the back of her throat, the thing between her legs. food disappears rather than becomes digested. her eyelids close over nothing, opening and summoning back sight in a dark creation. there is no birth in it, no joy, only a strange, occult surprise (*now i see*). no guarantees, no inhale, exhale, intake and debt fulfillment. now it's magic, not biology.

one night, a few weeks ago (SEISMOLOGICAL AGENCY DEADLOCKED OVER FAILURE TO IMPLEMENT NEW EMERGENCY STANDARDS: "THE MONEY JUST ISN'T THERE."), k tried to disprove her own fears. though it wasn't what she wanted, she asked bea to put her fingers inside her.

while in effect this not wanting was like being stone, k knew it wasn't the same thing. she thought of what was wrong with her as a sickness rather than a way of being, and she decided to heal through exposure therapy.

are you sure? asked bea.

desperate to be biological again, k begged her. *i want you inside me*, she insisted.

so, gentle and slow, bea tried and tried, but she couldn't do it. her fingers were stopped, blocked—no entry.

are you sure you want me to? said bea.

try just a little harder, said k.

i don't want to hurt you! said bea.

you won't, said k. but bea did hurt her, and k cried. bea's fingers couldn't go inside her because there was nowhere to go. that night, k slept in her binder again, wishing that she had one for her lower half, for her entire body.

3:14 a.m. k watches the ceiling stay motionless. is it emptiness (a balloon) or filledness (black sand) inside her? it's hard to tell, but it helps pass the time. *i'm more than my body*, she thinks. but this doesn't actually mean anything.

some fucking man touched me today. bea said it into her bowl of soup, her words disappearing into the steam.

what happened? said k. she set down her taco, split it open, and poured more hot sauce inside.

i don't know, bea said, shrugging. *just another man who felt like he needed to grab my ass.* she spooned in a mouthful, shoulders uncharacteristically hunched. casual is another kind of work.

k looked up. *really? what did you do?* she asked. *did you get in his face?*

of course not, said bea. *of course i didn't.*

why not?

because that's stupid. jerking away, sweat breaking out on the back of her neck, on her chest, like her mouth watering for nausea, embarrassed by the squeak that came from her throat, bea had hurried back to her building and rushed inside, not looking behind her, thinking only about getting to the stairwell. she took them two at a time, no eye contact with anyone, even those she knew; shoved open the door (TERRAFUTURES printed across the glass); and slid into her desk. still hot, wet under her arms, the ticking feeling of blood beneath her skin (*not a big deal, calm down*), wanting to call Mom and cry, wanting to call Claire and scream. why wasn't she used to it by now? in the bathroom, hyperventilating (on the sign: *with the amount of water used in a single flush, a family of four could—*). she wasted precious water on her face and hands, then returned to her desk, moist as a used napkin.

it's not stupid, k said, hot sauce dripping from her fingers. *you need to stand up to those guys. shame them publicly.*

back at her desk, where bea spends her days analyzing sexual-assault statistics in the Global South, watching over the years as climate slums transition into refugee camps before becoming prisons that eventually stop appearing on Google maps, she had played one of her favorite videos, UNBELIEVABLE EARTHQUAKE FOOTAGE FROM INDONESIA. finally, she had started to calm down.

that's just not how i handle it, bea replied. bea was used to bad attention from men; she understood that returning their aggression only made things worse.

well, maybe you should. k wiped her hand on a napkin. she sounded irritated.

i don't want to talk about it anymore. bea wanted to throw her soup against the wall, watch it bleed down the beige paint. *forget about it.*

i just worry about you, bea. i hate it when that shit happens to you.

yeah, said bea, her eyes riveted on the tabletop. *me too.*

they didn't talk for a long time, and their evening continued on, the space of time between dinner and bea's bed long and bleak, like a crowded beach on a hot, cloudless day.

THE NIGHT IT HAPPENED

so you're not from here, said the Woman in Black.

yet again, she had appeared next to k. she was holding something, but k wouldn't remember what it was. many different times in the future (IT'S THE END OF THE WORLD AS WE KNOW IT), k would recall this woman and her clothes and the way she held that something, whatever it was. she would not remember the Woman in Black's name, which she announced without being asked, like a man in a suit in a movie. but she was not a man or in a movie. she was a person in real life, and she was wearing the same clothes as k was.

no, k said, and escaped again. she found Glory in the kitchen.

so how do you know her? asked Glory. she leaned gracefully against the sink, the mistress of casual inquiry.

Glory and k met back when both were still trying to be boys. it had been several years, almost many, and since then Glory had moved onward, soldiering through a world of bullshit to get to where she was now. k had retreated back into her original gender, a version blurred by neglect: every six months or so, she revisited her intention to go to therapy, but there was somehow never enough money.

their first date had burned with tension, a sexual promise k couldn't put her (at the time, his) finger on. neither knew what happened in the 48 hours between that first date and their second, which ended with them standing on a dock, the long machinery of the ports looming above their heads. the black shape of the city trembled in the water, which shook the lighter, greyer black of the boats that crowded the ferry. they bickered about whether it was a tremor (this was back when the tremors were novel, still only occurring once or twice a week, a phenomenon to be discussed with other people), or just the natural movement of the Bay.

it was the first true conversation they'd had that evening, and it was pleasant but, anxious about the failure of this second date—its dearth of electricity and its glut of phone examination—k ruined the moment. she (at the time, he) tried to kiss Glory.

Glory smiled and pulled away. it broke the spell. still uncomfortable, though not as uncomfortable as they both already were, k in her first binder and Glory (back then, immaculately short-haired) with her nightmares of awakening like this in twenty years, of awakening like this in the morning, they began to laugh, their teeth shining in the yellow light, like the water that lapped the briny wood of the dock. when Glory had to go home, they took the long walk to Lake Merritt at a leisurely pace, and waved goodbye across the BART platform as the train carried her away.

now safely enmeshed in friendship, they told this story so often that it was worn smooth as polished jade. having discovered their perfect platonic affinity, they were practiced in embracing as they announced: *we were always gay for each other!* the two queens were now dykes, although unlike k and bea, Glory and her girlfriend were not monogamous, and never had been.

i don't know her, k said. she added her cup to the row that Glory was filling. *i met her here. tonight.*

y'all hitting it off.

no.

oh, come on, said Glory. *don't be weird.*

how am i being weird? asked k, looking over her shoulder. the Woman in Black was talking to some people by the couch, her hand resting on the side table where Ken's homemade seismometer squatted above a broken record player. she was probably cruising, the cruising type: broad shoulders, clear face, smiling too much, probably confusing k's flightiness for coy intrigue.

k believed that if she let herself behave like she really wanted to that she would revert to the tantrums of her childhood, becoming *too much*. this was why remaining in control of herself—of her expressions and speech and behavior—was so valuable to her. but when she was being watched—not in the way everybody was all the time, by cameras and security systems (SPACEX AND CORECIVIC TO PARTNER

FOR FIRST PRISON IN EARTH'S ORBIT), but by a fellow queer—as she was tonight, it wasn't easy to remain in control. there was something about it (a bug in a bell jar) that sapped her ability to stay calm, straight-backed, distant in the way that she took pride in. instead, her wrists and legs slackened, and when she caught her own reflection in mirrors and glass, she saw a stranger. she felt herself relaxing as she devolved, weakening, listening to herself laughing constantly, even when nothing funny had been said. self-aware as prey, she felt her back arch and her jaw clench. the Woman in Black saw her as clearly as Glory did.

but the Woman in Black was not Glory. she wore leather boots. she had the look of someone who never went to the gym but played outside whenever she could, building things and climbing trees. she was thick-lashed as a teenage boy.

fine, said Glory. *don't talk to me about it. fuck me for being interested*.

interested, repeated k dully, pulling out her phone. bea had texted her. k read the message without unlocking her screen. we're here. on your way? k had meant to leave at around this time, but she decided to stay a little longer; she would get back to bea in a few minutes. she put her phone in her pocket and snatched the bottle from Glory's hand, topping off her cup a little more.

thanks for the help, snapped Glory. ever the hostess (a natural offshoot of the nurturer), she picked up the tray of drinks, amused but less so than she would have been five years ago, or even last summer. *you're a dog*, she'd once said to k, *and sometimes i worry what that says about me* (a tattoo Glory had been considering for a minute: *femme4femme4ever*). she left k in the kitchen, walking back to where Ken stood in his clot of friends, his laughter echoing off their bodies.

k turned away. she didn't care if Glory was staring her down. there were other eyes in the room. she could name almost everyone at this party, even if she couldn't say they were a friend. over on the couch was Jae, who k met in a community-college class she eventually dropped out of (a prereq for a coding bootcamp. Jae completed it, but was still paying off the tuition by working at a bike shop). Sibyl, who used to bike for k's company but was now in herb school, was luring an orange cat out from behind the fridge with her shoelace. next to the altar was Arianna, Glory's partner (a rope of black pearls from an estate sale around her neck; *Dyke Drama* tattooed on her left ankle), who paid the bills by nannying for techies.

Arianna and Glory had been together for years. they were the dykes to whom k compared herself and bea, the gold standard of partnership. the two of them didn't argue much, but when they did, it was with an extremity that k felt was indicative of their commitment. k saw the shrieking, the plate-throwing, the threats to leave and take the cat with them, as signs of maturity. they rarely argued about their other lovers, but about the things to which k saw herself and bea one day ascending: rent and medical bills, family to whom one wasn't out, who was going to miss work to take the cat for her shots.

bea texted k again: just let me know when you're here love

k read the text, put her phone in her pocket, then pulled it back out to read it again. she didn't need to look around her to know where the Woman in Black was, had always known where she was in relation to her body from the first moment she saw her. k knew that she was watching her, too, just as Glory was watching her.

k put her phone away.

MONOGAMY

bea understands that with k, there is always going to be risk.

she's kind of like a shy Shane. that was how Claire once described her, after meeting k for the first time that morning. they had all gone for breakfast together, where k had gamely withstood Claire's polite barrage of questions, dizzy from the attention and hungover from the scent of bea's bed. it was only when they were saying goodbye that bea realized she had been nervous for her best friend and her new partner to meet.

except for Shane was *kind of shy, huh?* Claire went on.

it's not like she's slept with everybody. and anyway, everyone has slept with everyone, said bea. bea had not slept with many people. *it's not really the same thing.*

i just mean that being, like, super free and poly and sleeping with everyone is her thing, said Claire. *and if you don't want to have an open relationship, well ...*

ABOUT BEA

bea thinks of herself as grounded and down-to-earth, a classic Taurus whose sensibility is rooted in The Natural. she likes to plant things. she enjoys long walks, preferring not to swim or to bike or to climb, but rather to run, to dance, to bend her body along the ground, drawing her sureness from crystals and votives (k teases her, but takes comfort in these artifacts, too), from the soft geometry of succulents and apartments built low to the ground, or beneath it.

when she had been at school, bea had majored in geology. she had signed up for her classes expecting leisurely slideshows of rich shoveled soil, pixel-textured rock formations heaving and twisting in ponderous array, and perhaps in more advanced courses, film of active volcanoes in slow boil; the study of what could be surmised about other earths orbiting other suns. in retrospect, she doesn't know what she had planned to do with her degree; the only thing more unrealistic than someone like her getting a Ph.D. was someone like her using higher education to become something other than an accountant or a nurse.

luckily, she hadn't needed to decide. near the end of her fourth semester, there was an opportunity at work, and she took it—money being more important than education, the exchange rate between the two having dropped off considerably since bea's parents had been her age (DNC REFUSES TO CONDEMN PRIVATIZATION OF THE MILITARY).

the position was in administration at a mid-size nonprofit, and bea is still there, Monday through Friday, always fighting to keep her hours below forty-five. she keeps a small crystal in the right corner of her desk, a thing to touch with her index finger—too rough to stroke—unpolished, veined, not quite transparent but warm when the light catches it, a hardened fusion to illuminate her way, though it's gathered a film of dust since she started bookmarking earthquake videos.

bea doesn't plan on returning to school. she has her crystal (a descendent of her first touchstone, a thrilling glob of hematite, which was confiscated by a nun in elementary school (*a false idol*)) when she needs it, and she remembers a few things from her classes, enough to be slightly better-informed about the materials of the planet, of rock at its most dense and at its most diffuse—stone, dirt, dust, infinitesimal particular debris—than the average person, including k, who took her to the California Academy of Sciences, a surprise field trip for her lovely scientist, in honor of their one-month anniversary.

bea loved the geological exhibit, but her strongest memories are of the earthquake room, a small enclosure designed to look like the middle-class home of another century, the kind with a white-picket fence. framed by its false bay windows was a vinyl cityscape, and every five minutes, that cityscape underwent The Great San Francisco Earthquake of 1906, rocking the middle-class home to the delight of the people inside it.

for bea and k, the simulation (apocryphal crockery rattling, mysterious klaxons, lurid automated voices, the startled screams of a real child) had been a Moment:

falling into each other, copping feels, laughing, cackling even, bea snorting and k losing her balance and falling, dragging bea with her, and then they found they couldn't stand again, they were so out of breath. when the room finally stopped moving, they seized the wainscoting for balance, pulling their jellied legs from the door, throwing final glances at the blue-checked window drapes, the round tank brimming with hard plastic water and petrified fish, before stepping back out into the main gallery, still laughing.

on the wall outside the earthquake room were photographs of the city blown up big enough to see from across the gallery. there it was: San Francisco after the fire, a city annihilated, an ashen nothing, flattened and smoking from Market Street to the Sunset District, collapsed, burned out, the black-clad survivors crowding Alamo Square in monochrome disbelief. as they looked, craning their necks to take in all of it, their laughter slowly faded away.

i can't believe it, bea finally said. she clutched the handle of her backpack in her right hand, its straps dragging on the floor. she thought she had known, she thought she had understood, but this catastrophe was nothing like the ones she was familiar with, not the four-alarm arson fires started by West Oakland landlords, or NorCal dam failures that took out rice farmers and meth labs with the same senseless cruelty. it was so much bigger, blindly indiscriminate, and beyond the control of humans to prevent or mitigate. written on a placard below all the photos was a paragraph that began with, *The Cascadia Subduction Zone: Predicting the Next Disaster.*

so, you think we'll survive the Big One? asked k. she threw her arm around bea and started to laugh again.

THE PANTRY

a long, deep closet lined with shelves full of cans, mason jars filled with oats, dried beans, rice, chia seeds, and ground coffee, a Cuisinart mixer shoved into a corner, a mammoth plastic tub of smaller Tupperware containers (hulking clear insect laden with young), the back wall the least full and the most empty, with a shelf, penultimate from the bottom, that juts out, thick enough to support her body, so k puts her there, fingers tracing the leather and the denim, the belt loops, the cool metal button, the zipper, the briefs coming down with the pants, a flash—a moment empathizing, feeling her warm skin on the chill painted wood—then shoving the denim down over her thighs, caught, loaded, trapped over them and above her shoes, running her hips, skin softly radiating around them, the give of thigh, soft and hard, the blue-black shadow high over her groin, joining, thin and dark as thread, going up and out a little below her navel, tracing the line, the hairs with her tongue, wedging her legs open with her left elbow, using her right arm to balance her weight, her hand around behind her lower back. pure silence but breathing (*did they close the door?*), controlling herself, willing her mouth to stay along her edge, going up the walls of her thighs, longing to bite, staying, encircling, her hand on k's neck, her hand supporting her weight behind her, a strange balance, her legs pinioned by her pants, held apart by k's shoulders, k's arms braced, k's mouth soaking her hair, the small, granular texture and hot skin beneath: spice, bacteria, heat, chemistry, avoiding the point, circling like a drain, building to a head, a heat, a heart at the head of her cunt, her hand wrenching k's scalp.

THE GOOD DAY

they woke up early and at the same time, but they stayed in bed, twisting the sheets, whispering, clearing throats. bea's comforter was slightly too heavy but the unheated apartment (*Women Are Beautiful* on a print on one wall; *Your Cops Won't Save You* over a crowd of masked people, all in black) was too cold to allow even a wrist or a shoulder out from beneath it. they staved off breakfast for almost an hour, curled up in shared sweat and faded linen and citron.

when they were hungry enough, bea wrapped herself in her grandmother's fleece bathrobe and led k, draped in the comforter, to the kitchen. they made French toast and black tea, slipping in their socks over the linoleum. they ate slowly and a little too much, laughing and licking each other's fingers. they left the dirty plates in the sink.

after k taught bea how to ride a bike, they started riding together (although bea didn't like it as much as she pretended to. this was one of her secrets), k on her Peugeot, bea on the bike k helped her build. wobbling over the sidewalk and into the street, they remembered the time they went to the shop to get bea her first helmet. there had been only men working there, all of them nice except for the owner, and bea and k had laughed at his condescension to his face and later, sharing a cigarette on the stoop, laughed again at his arrogant pate and fatless, hairless calves.

it took a long time to get to the Point, but they felt like they could go on riding forever. they locked up their bikes in the parking lot and struck out across the rocky peninsula, but they didn't see any other people until they got to the beach at its westernmost tip, where a pack of dogs—dainty purebreds; gamboling retrievers; one hulking, matted hybrid—raced across the sand to meet them.

they could have scouted ahead around the outcropping to where crumbling concrete obelisks and short scrubby trees tumbled toward the surfless waterline, to where, perhaps, the dog's owners might have been found observing the horizon and the hateful city that razored through it, while they waited for their animals to tire themselves out.

instead, they ran to the dogs, slowing only to snatch up sticks to hurl for the ones that cared, and those that did returned with them at breakneck speed, all rolling eyes and flapping lips, their feet somehow hitting the earth before their jaws did. they slammed into one another, the animals tipping over bea and k with their low bodies and blunted claws. laughing, they extended their hands to be smelled, and the dogs rejoiced, racing and feinting and tackling one another in excitement, welcoming these new pack members and their odors of tea and WD-40, their brachiating arms that rubbed ears and threw sticks and, a few minutes later, tossed the almost-new tennis ball shyly presented by the shepherd, as if it all wasn't temporary.

maybe this was staged, said k, patting the flank of the dancing hybrid. *maybe we're on a reality show for happy people.*

they kept running. they ran until their eyes burned with water and their lungs ached, and the dogs still wanted to play. they finally stopped, just to catch their breath, and turned to the view—the city and the bridges and the little islands, k rubbing a grain of sand from her eye—but when they turned back, the dogs had sprinted away, their prints disappearing into the dry dunes that faded into the scrub, and they were gone. with huge, dumbfounded eyes, with gaping mouths and more laughter, bea and k turned to one another, arms extended, unbelieving, howling with the unspoken question.

they found their bikes exactly as they left them, and Yelp knew of a vegan café that was nearby. they splurged on thick sandwiches and ate them as they lounged in enormous pleather chairs, flipping through real, printed newspapers, a crossword on every page.

when they were done, they got back on their bikes, prepared to absorb the remainder of the day beneath them: stubborn bea attempting an impossible hill, and on its steep descent, k throwing her hands over her head while bea screamed. *stop that!* bea ordered, but she laughed, too.

they led each other down and around the bike trails and parklets and sloping neighborhoods of emaciated Victorians and broad Buddhist temples, past stuccos mid-face-lift and the smoking remains of firebombed condos, past the verdant sewage lake where waterbirds—glorious and iridescent-throated—sipped through the algae, along smooth, winding mainways choked with other cyclists and leisurely lights, over the piss-stained pavement through encampments of tarpaulin and blankets where people (smoking, cooking, talking) waited for something, past piebald dog parks and incense-scented corner stores and mattresses surrounded by fruity piles of refuse, all the way to the overpass by bea's apartment where a hundred candles still burned in witness beneath an unfinished mural, and where they dismounted, finally, to look at the bloodstains.

it was the daunting pre-twilight, when time always felt a little wasted. the dirty dishes were still there, but so was the bed, and they got back inside it until the sun was completely gone, bea's whole fist inside k, a thing they both knew, knowledge just for them, a moment of knowing each other completely, *i am you*, *we are us*, inside, and your pleasure, mine.

GOING ONLINE

k knows what to expect once the ad goes live. no matter where she posts it, or for whom, the deluge of responses from men will be immediate and overwhelming.

in the past, when she posted under m4m (crew cut, binder, small-gauged earrings: less masculine than she currently is, but more manly in that she sought to pass, and often did), even when she came right out and said it in the ad, *i'm a boy with a pussy, i'm a transgender man, i'm a dude with girl parts,* for clarity, for safety, there were some men who were still surprised, especially the older ones. as if they really hadn't read any part of the ad, hadn't even examined the headless, groinless photo for clues—and there were plenty, if you knew what to look for.

it had occurred to k, as she wrote this new ad, that she never actually met any women this way, even when she wanted to. all her responses had been from men, all her meetings were with men. as a former man, or a person formerly trying to be a man, these ads were a man's pastime, a man's secret communication with other men, a man's friendly, impersonal fuck. even when the men she met decided she was a woman, and she corrected them; even when the men she met decided she was a woman, and she didn't.

writing this new ad, k feels out of practice, as if finding other people online is a skill, and perhaps it is. but this time her goal was completely different, her ad unique from all the others she has ever made. even so, she had expected to feel more steady in this context, which once belonged to her, after all.

but it has changed since k grew her hair a little, dropped the paperwork, stopped defending her pronouns (when she met bea, bea did not ask what k's were, and k did not tell her, and so bea used *she/her* for k, and k liked how it felt to relax into assumption). though she continued to think of herself as not quite female long after she had given up on surgery and hormones and the whole thing, online cruising felt less and less *hers*, and the last time had been bad, bad enough that it would still probably have been her last time (another attempt at canceling out a long, disappointing weekend of too much booze at grinding, blaring parties where she stood until her legs ached and still nothing happened, awakening at 6 the next morning on her only day off by the crash into sobriety, the alcohol oozing through her bowels like rotten food, her skin clammy and parched after two nights of cruising on methy blow or off molly, alone except for whoever she fucked in the bathroom or made out with by the ATM because Glory and Arianna had a fight and stayed in, and Ken went home with a guy from Grindr before 10, leaving her in a dark room overseen by a vanity DJ whose creative urge far exceeded their talent, with no one in her phone she wanted to text), even if she hadn't met bea.

after a weekend like that, the last tool in k's arsenal was to resurrect the old w4m standby (exact specifications re: cock size and appearance, but not STI status, re: grooming habits but not contagion—*and do you have anything to party with?*), add an updated body shot, and then wait for the emails to come. and they did, almost all of them incoherent or stupid or terrifying, including the ones she responded to, including the one she had responded to and managed to still regret.

k expects to feel the earth shake when she presses PUBLISH, but of course, it doesn't. the tremors never happen when you think they will.

THE PAST

at the beginning of their relationship, bea asked k about hustling only once or twice before k got angry.

i'm sorry! said bea. she felt guilty for delving into something that was obviously painful (*Greg*). *i didn't know it bothered you.*

she wondered how she even knew about k's old job in the first place. she didn't remember that Glory told her, unaware that k hadn't wanted bea to know.

i'm sorry, i thought she knew! exclaimed Glory, throwing up her hands. like most poised people, the loss of her composure embarrassed everyone.

it's fine, said k, gritting her teeth. *it's fine.*

it must have been traumatic for k, thought bea, or else she wouldn't mind talking about it. did the trauma lie in the fact of a female selling sex, which was always regrettable and pitiable in the eyes of the world? or was it in a particular experience, a bad thing that had happened? did it have something to do with a life (three years of maleness and four months on T) that k no longer lived?

just because bea didn't mention it anymore didn't mean that they could ignore it, of course: it seemed like everyone they knew sold sex, or used to, or dated someone who did. it was inevitable that it came up, and when it did, k would feel bea looking at her (whether or not bea truly was), and feel the cold grind of panic.

BEA'S BODY

what are you worried about

right now? it takes k almost fifteen minutes to answer bea's
text. she's on a delivery all the way across the city from the
Marina down to the Lower Mission.

in general. bea replies right away. she is at home, in her bed.
the cat is on the windowsill, gazing out into the darkness.
as bea waits for k to respond, a dog tries a few interrogative
howls on the other side of the fence outside her window, and
the cat's ears swivel to the sound.

why do you ask

because you're not sleeping, texts bea. i know you're not

k braces her left leg on the pedal, supporting her weight, and
her bike's, on her right foot. she thinks for a moment before
responding, typing slowly. beneath her, a tremor begins,
startling a handful of pigeons into flight.

i have insomnia. i always have. k's dad had insomnia, too,
all through her childhood. she doesn't know if he still does.

bea sets her phone down and pushes herself back into the pillows. k can't hide her exhaustion, as much as she wants to. bea has been trying to talk to her about it for weeks, for almost as long as they haven't had sex. she's beginning to wonder if she's crazy, if she's really just horny and projecting everything else. at a loss, she tries to keep it simple.

well, i'm worried, she texts.

bea's care warms k; here it is, a moment to melt. on bea's side, the ellipses of work in progress appears.

i'm sorry i—k begins, when a group of men appear on the sidewalk beside her, reaching toward her bike. she tells them to fuck off, and they retaliate, their figures tall and handsome and clean, using her own words against her.

phone still in hand, k pedals away, fast, gunning for Van Ness. the figures and their laughter only carry as far as the next block, but they'll be around, always a few steps behind. she looks down at her phone again, but it's hard to text and ride this fast. she deletes her initial reply—too complicated—and starts over.

don't be, texts k, her eyes bouncing between the screen and oncoming traffic.

bea tosses her phone away and picks up her book again. she wants the cat to come to her, and makes a kissing noise, but the cat ignores it, her eyes still lost in the nighttime. outside, the dog has stopped barking. on her side of the Bay, there hasn't been a tremor since this morning.

*lookig 4 a women ilk u into my thing a little freak u kno sned
more pix?*

*where do u live also any face shots to make sure your not a butter
face lol*

*interested bt dont have medical records (no insurance rn) can we
meet and talk. what s your number*

how does k know from content alone that her responses—a
few dozen in the first hour—all came from men, even the
ones that profess otherwise, even though she posted in
w4w and stated she preferred a woman (or any other non-
male person, though she hadn't come out and said this),
even though what she is asking is bizarre, and couldn't be
anything other than a joke, a weird bot, a performance-art
piece, the actions of a troll with nothing better to do? it
seems that the internet, the place where everything is gotten
and begotten (including the prescription medication k has
taken off and on, for years, for the sores that got her into this
situation), runneth over.

k refreshes the page after every new email, and more bolded headers appear, her poor inbox a pastiche of misspelled homonyms, transparent lies, and fresh spam (DONATE NOW #BUILDTHEWALL). she doesn't want to be repulsed—these men are just being themselves, after all—but she is, even though she is the one who is a liar. she is the one who wants this horrible thing in the first place.

ABOUT BEA

the last time bea visited her mom, it was just the two of them. the apartment was empty, not even a cat padding the hardwood between the tiny foyer and the French doors that opened into Mom's mattress-size bedroom. when Greg died, Mom was between boyfriends, and rather than find a roommate, she'd put his things in storage and moved.

being alone with her mom felt strange to bea. perhaps this was because, in her memories, this rarely happened. bea had been an only child, but someone else besides her mom always seemed to be around: a live-in boyfriend; Mom's best friend, Patti, sleeping on their couch for the summer; and then later on, Uncle Greg.

you can do that? said bea. *he didn't go to one of those places?*

of course you can, said Mom. *lots of people do it at home. my dad did. your dad's parents, too.*

but that was so long ago, said bea. *it seems like it would be different now. like there would be a law.*

Mom shook her head, still stirring. the dominoes hissed like snakes, rubbing against each other like marble knuckles. bea had never met Dad's mom and dad, though she had a photo of them in a shoebox under her bed. the colors had faded over time, hinting at a former vibrancy. the people in it sat in folding chairs on a slab of concrete surrounded by dust, their hands folded across their laps, their bifocals identical. bea couldn't envision her grandparents outside the photo any more than she could summon the homes they'd once lived in (bathrooms she'd never seen, bedrooms she couldn't imagine) back in Tucson, a city she'd only visited as a very small child.

her only memories of that place were of heat, back before heat meant anything (ORLEANS PARISH APPOINTS RELOCATION COUNCIL: "IT'S THE BEGINNING OF THE END."), and of hiding from the brightness of the sky in someone's arms. whose? a nameless relative whose bleached hair and long, inviolable acrylics bea still dreams about, a history just for herself. later, when she asked Dad who that woman had been, describing her beauty, her artificiality, her soft, warm arms, he screwed up his mouth, looked up at the sky, and shrugged.

did you see him die? asked bea. Greg had never gone with them to visit Dad's family, of course. he and Dad hated each other.

Mom looked up. *no*, she said. *no, he went in his sleep.* she did not indicate if this had been upsetting, if she would have preferred it to be another way (dominoes swirling like a galaxy, audio like chiming snow in a children's video game). until he died, Mom had only ever talked to Greg, not about him.

but i might as well have seen it happen, she went on. *i saw everything else. his body changed. it happened so fast, you wouldn't believe it.* contemplatively, she examined a tile, its white back gleaming under the lamplight. *his legs were so thin you could snap them in half.*

the black pearls of her own tiles swam before bea's eyes. why did people always describe weakness with violence? why not go the other way? *his legs were so thin you could tend to them. his legs were so thin you could swaddle them in velvet. his legs were so thin you could wrap your arms around them and hold them until they got better.*

but then, why should she care? she hated Greg.

NOT ALL MEN

once, bea said: *i don't know. sometimes i feel weird just dismissing
all of them. they're not all bad.*

the vast majority is enough, k had responded. her indignation
sounded like pride. perhaps she was unaware of the bedrock
emotion beneath it, wrapped around the knowledge that
bea had loved men as a woman, and perhaps would again;
and that bea loved k, who was not fully a woman, which
meant that she could only be a man, which was not true (but
how could it not be?) (and beneath that, even further, even
deeper, the hatred of men that had nothing to do with the
things they had done, but the things they *were* and could be,
effortlessly, naturally, that belonged to them as definitely as
k belonged nowhere).

looking embarrassed, bea went on walking in silence, their
discussion—the exact subject of which k forgot long ago—
put to death. that she'd been able to silence bea had surprised
k almost as much as bea's apology for men.

just who do you think you are? asks Glory. three threads of hair
stick to her throat, a rivulet along a tendon that glows black

and then gold when she turns toward the sun that's been split down the middle by the Lake. they stretch their legs on the curved bike racks planted in the grass, stifling yawns. *i never met anyone as boy-crazy as you*, she goes on, *and i know Ken.*

i don't like them as people, says k. *i just want to fuck them sometimes. it's different.*

uh-huh.

i know it's not rational.

your attraction to men or your hatred of them? asks Glory.

k laughs. *both*, she says.

you're right, it's not rational, says Glory. *you really can't see why bea doesn't hate every last one of them? i can.*

but they've hurt her (she pauses and then, to generalize, keeps going) *as much as they've hurt anyone*, says k. *if you aren't only attracted to them, why bother at all? straight women, i guess, are stuck, but if you're queer, you can just stay away from them forever if you want.*

like you do? says Glory.

you know what i mean. i mean, why would you date them if you didn't have to?

i wonder what a straight girl would think about that, says Glory. the straps of her sports bra are narrower than the neck of her tee shirt. they frame her throat, a shimmering expanse behind the thin gold chain she always wears. *or a bi girl, for that matter.*

i'm right though, aren't i? even if you liked men, wouldn't you stay with women, and, like, other queers? you'd still be with Arianna, wouldn't you?

you know, that's an interesting question, says Glory.

i'm right, aren't i?

i've never once been attracted to a man, ever. including you, when you were one, i have to admit. so lez it's not funny, says Glory, chuckling. she kneels to tighten her shoelaces. k mirrors her. *well, Tom Hardy does make me wonder, but he's the exception that proves the rule, i guess.*

gross. but k laughs.

oh, like you wouldn't sit on his dick in your time of need, says Glory, pushing k's shoulder. now they laugh together, bouncing on their heels.

k realizes her sweat is almost dry, and she glances at her watch. they've gotten lost in their conversation and now their warm-up has been for nothing (tagged on the concrete: THESE FAGGOTS KILL FASCISTS).

ugh, says Glory. *we're never gonna get abs at this rate.* she suddenly launches into a sprint, darting away from the bike racks.

just pretend there are men chasing you, shouts k, running after her.

BEA'S BODY

no, k says, pulling away, immersing herself in the comforter, tucking her hair behind her ear. *no*.

bea pulls away in the other direction, but puts out her hand, trying to touch k's hair as she does.

i'm sorry, bea says.

i'm sorry, k echoes. *i can't really handle that right now*.

a few minutes ago, when bea put her arm around her shoulder and kissed her, k thought that maybe she could do it this time. bea removed both their clothes for them, trying to be sensual, but gentle, playful and calm, trying to make it so that there could be no danger, no fear.

but there was no part of bea's body that did not remind k of her own and its failure. there was no part of her body that could be safe, nor was there a position—fucker, fuckee, soft sapphic middle devoid of power dynamics—in which she could escape from the mirror and reminder of bea. tonight, k will not fuck, nor will she be fucked—not in a stone way, a state that had come and gone for years, but in a different way, a way that had been born with the sore.

bea pulls the comforter over their bodies. she wants to say, *i just want you to feel good*, but she doesn't (has she forgotten about honesty?), although there have been times before, as far inside k as she could go, her knee between k's thighs, k's head thrown back over the pillow, eyes closed, panting, that bea felt as if she would fuck even deeper, and it wouldn't matter if that was what k wanted because what she was, she herself, was k's desire, as well as her own. *you're mine*, she would whisper, and when they came out from under, when the orgasms were gone and the ideas of the next thing, which oughtn't exist during sex but sometimes do, had taken back over again, bea was the same as she was before, burying herself in k's neck so she didn't risk looking into her eyes for too long and betraying herself.

bea decides not to say anything. instead, she puts her arm over k's body, and k does not resist. bea wants to look at her, but senses that she shouldn't. she closes her eyes (*i love her and that's enough*) and loses herself in Tōhoku, Valdivia, Mexico City. k can't close her eyes, because then she won't know it if bea decides to open hers again, decides to look at her, and she doesn't want to be seen.

queerness is exposure. when people know that you're queer, they know that you desire, that you pervert, that you fuck. (and people always know k is queer, no matter what gender they think she is.) being straight is neutrality. being queer is indelible, for you and for those you touch. being queer is infection. k wants quarantine.

GOING ONLINE

not a female but i can do everything you want.
if you're interested, text me at **xxx xxx xxxx**

k studies the email: short, direct, lucid. threatless, imageless, polite. no dick pic, no demands. she weighs its domain and the hour of its arrival. she allows herself to imagine the writer. he is white, she decides. older but not old. not attractive, but not ugly, either.

such a normal email. too normal. anyone who bothers to project a veneer of normalcy in the pursuit of such perversion must be seriously sick. the only question is, how will it manifest with this man? that is, how is he different from the others who have responded, whose expression of their desires were more repugnant than the desires themselves?

this matters because the risk of rape or murder or exposure is higher with someone like this, a man whose perversity isn't concealed, brought out on a leash in the security of a throwaway email address, but whose behavior in his real life—work; marriage to a cis woman; fatherhood to biological children; "interests"; leisure activities; regular moderate exercise; paying bills on time; business trips; long, thoughtful moments, hands perched on a shopping cart in front of an enormous cold case, deliberating between different brands of the same flavor of ice cream—is identical to his behavior as he scrolls through forums where people and bots pretending to be human females advertise their temporary availability and interest in human males for semi-legal (or semi-illegal) acts of which the majority of the world would profess to be horrified.

k knows this from experience, knows that for this man, in both spheres, there is no dissembling or shame. she also knows that her question is one that can't be answered, at least not until she meets him: what is wrong with this person?

THE BIG ONE

the woman who sells bea her coffee is dying.

her cheeks are creamed with pale down (mammalian lichen).
she wears fingerless gloves and flannel in the summertime,
though the layers can't conceal her emaciation or the tight
shine of her skin. freckled like a teenager and probably a year
or two older than bea (bea can't know this for sure, but feels
it to be true), the woman who sells bea her coffee doesn't
talk much. bea always talks to her, as she likes to do when
people and places become a part of her routine. the talking
reassures her and, she hopes, reassures those people—her
dentist, the maintenance man at her office, the woman who
sells bok choy by the 12th Street BART Station—she sees
on a regular basis: *i'm a good addition.*

the café is hip, because coffee is so expensive these days
that only nice places can afford to sell it anymore. there are
air planters on the walls and exotic fruits for sale, organic
baubles of unbelievable price that make an espresso seem
reasonable in comparison. where once there may have
been a corkboard with multilingual job listings and flyers
for punk shows is a narrow shelf layered with slick 3x5s

advertising New American Street Festivals and Millennial Wine Tastings and DisruptrCon. but a cup of coffee once or twice a week is bea's great indulgence, a luxury she finds harder and harder to justify with each passing year.

the staff doesn't wear name tags, but bea knows the woman's name, her eyes drifting up when the word, *Amy,* is called out by the man washing dishes or the queer steaming milk. considering the chicness of her surroundings, her clothes are surprisingly drab (worn Under Armor and cheap cotton tank tops; a glossy puffed vest, shimmering like damp; a thin turtleneck gathered under her ears, the elastic not strong enough to cling to her body), but her fingernails—short, manicured, today matte cobalt, tomorrow scarlet lined with marzipan—are always impeccable.

when bea complimented them for the tenth time, Amy finally favored her with a reply: *i do them myself.* grateful, bea tipped her double. she remembers when the exchange happened because it fell on the day that Hayward had another > 4.0 quake (POTUS THANKS POLICE, SAYS POST-HURRICANE LOOTERS "WERE ASKING FOR IT"), the second of the year, which she noted in the spreadsheet she keeps, irregularly, on local seismic activity. though she follows the news religiously, checking the Seismic Update multiple times a day, she feels a revulsion for examining the hard data too closely. they're exact and yet altogether useless, since they can't tell her exactly *when* the Big One is going to happen, and that's the only information that counts as far as bea is concerned. sometimes she feels that if she could only know *when* it's going to happen, she wouldn't be afraid of it anymore. sometimes she thinks she's just looking for reasons to be afraid. whatever the truth is, she figures it has to do with feeling safe.

what had happened to Amy that she was not allowed to feel safe? how was it different from what has happened to bea? bea wonders this of all women, except for k; it doesn't occur to her to wonder about k like that, in much the same way it doesn't occur to her to fear mass shootings, or the Bay Bridge collapsing into the water, unless as a direct consequence of the Big One, the only tragedy she is moved by, the only event she can anticipate and yet fail to plan for (no bugout bags, no freshwater hoarding, no CPR course), refusing to even keep her spreadsheet updated, doing nothing other than consume useless information online, like a pig at a trough full of poison.

Amy never wears shirts with words or images, or buttons with slogans, or jewelry, except for the anonymous silver rings lined up behind her perfect fingernails. none of her coworkers talk to her that bea ever sees, except to verify roasts and *are we out of oat milk?* bea knows nothing about her except what she can observe in the three to five minutes it takes to get her coffee. that, and the fact that she is dying, which is something that anyone could know just by looking at her.

like everyone else who can see Amy, bea speculates and pities, trying and failing to tamp down her presumption as she weighs the components of her own past and structures a formula, to find X being the goal—X itself being the event, condition, result, incident that separated her, bea, handing over her money, from her, Amy, taking it in her fingers, careful not to touch bea's, careful with the paper cup and compostable lid, careful with the crisp white receipt.

what is between us? wonders bea, as if it could be just one thing, or even a series of them. (our lives are not accumulations, they're universes; we're not equations, we're dreams). *why her and not me? why is she dying? why am i* not *dying?* is Amy sadder, sicker, more afraid? more sensitive, more damaged? more unlucky, more disappointed, more predisposed? more punished, more endangered, more raped? the possibilities are a mobile of existence in the air around bea's head, wavering, floating, moving, one series her own and one Amy's. there is one for her mother and one for Claire and one for Glory, all of them cantilevering, dangling, all in imbalance. (where is k's mobile?) by taking control, does one sacrifice the future? which is better to have, or worse to lose?

thank you, says bea, dropping her change in the tip jar.

mhm, says Amy.

AFTER IT HAPPENED

what would you do?

you cannot ask me that question, says Glory.

why not?

because, says Glory, *i wouldn't have fucked up in the first place.*

oh, come on.

i wouldn't. i love you but that was some stupid bro bullshit.

i know, says k. *i know.*

don't ask me what i would do, says Glory. *ask me what you should do.*

k laughs.

i am serious, says Glory. *you never ask anyone for help. i have to force it on you. but i actually give really good advice.*

i know, says k again. *but i don't think i should get advice for this. it's something i have to do myself. like i don't deserve advice.*

that's an interesting perspective.

i wonder what bea would do.

you know, by saying that, says Glory, shifting her weight as she selects another pencil—Topaz—from the mason jar, *i feel like you're trying to move the blame onto her.*

what? where did you get that?

when you say that, Glory goes on, pressing the pencil onto the paper and shading, in soft, minute lines, the cat's long, cape-like jacket, *it makes it seem like cheating is something bea might conceivably to do you. puts it in the realm of possibility. calls it into being.* she presses harder, and the lines darken. k is still holding the first pencil she took from the jar. her book is open but there aren't any colors on it.

and if you feel like it was something that bea could ever do, it becomes something that bea might *have done, or would do*, says Glory. she appears to be intensely focused on the cape. *that's what it feels like to me, anyway.*

that's not what i meant, says k. her eyes are hot. she feels a warmth, an itchiness, on her skin, and has all day, and the day before, like she hasn't showered in a week, like when she still had the long hair her dad wouldn't let her cut and the only time she let it down and felt it on her back was when she had to wash it and it hung, thick and humid and sweet-smelling, down her shoulders, invading under her ears and below her skull, a smothering nest beneath her head. when she was 16 she left home and moved in with a friend she'd met at the pizza parlor where they worked, and the friend had cut her hair for her with the scissors that came with her mom's knife set. k had wanted to dig it out, all of it, everything that was there at the base of her skull and even deeper: the steaming, matted clot, the hot underside of being awake with that weight always bearing down, and watching, too, watching her be ugly and strange and wrong.

i know, says Glory. she set down the pencil and shifted her weight again so that she was facing k. she reached out and took k's knee, rubbing hard through the denim. *i just wanted to point that out to you.*

i can't believe it, says k. *i never want to do this shit and then i do.* she rubs her eye sockets, her body deep in the couch pillows.

at some level, you do, though, says Glory. *or you wouldn't do it.*

i don't know. fuck, sometimes i feel like i can't control it.

like a sex addict? asks Glory.

no, says k. *i don't know. i should be poly.*

yeah, says Glory, *because you never fucked up when you weren't monogamous, right?*

k knows she doesn't expect an answer. Glory goes on.

so, she says. *did you talk to her?*

who?

her. that person, says Glory.

k jerks her hands away, her emptied eye sockets full of white. *no. i'm not going to, either.*

why not?

why not? it was a fucking mistake! it was fucked up. and if bea doesn't find out from somebody, i am going to have to tell her. that's hard enough to live with.

Glory rubs k's knee some more, leaning her head on the fist she's propped on the coffee table. her velvet skirt is the same dark red as the swirling paisley rug. on the wall is the print she gave k for her birthday: PROTECT TRANS YOUTH.

okay, k says, *i have another question. don't get mad.*

Glory laughs.

i don't want you to get upset.

and you're still gonna ask it? says Glory.

please?

Glory sighs. *okay*, she says.

remember Janessa? asks k.

she takes her hand off k's knee. *you think i forgot that bitch?* says Glory.

well, what if you'd never found out? or found out way later? could you have made it work with her, if you hadn't known what she did?

i knew you were gonna bring her up.

is this fucked up to ask? i really want to know.

your rude ass.

you told me you wanted to give me advice.

Glory sighs. *Janessa*, she says. k can tell she is thinking, seriously considering the question, has of course considered it before, has spent sleepless nights on it, on her younger self. she had just come out and had never been with another woman before. Janessa, older and experienced and beautiful, treated her like a princess.

(k will never admit to Glory that she hadn't liked Janessa because she wanted to be the only boy in Glory's life, be the one to take care of her in the way a boy takes care of a girl he loves, but Janessa, a carpenter with silky eyelashes who stood three inches taller than k, was Glory's everything. it was the first time k had ever been jealous.)

up until she went and fucked a straight girl. and then she left Glory for that straight girl (*like every masc.* k remembered Glory saying this a few years later, before suddenly shaking her head. *sorry, baby,* she said, sighing. *you know what i mean*). not long after their breakup, Glory saw them together at some dance party, Janessa's arm around the straight girl (petite and blond, natural tits, bourgie basic-bitch outfit), the two of them sharing a martini glass, and Glory—hot waves of grinding humiliation—felt her body beneath her clothes in relief, like a statue carved into a wall, trapped and exposed. she fled to the bathroom until k came to tell her, an hour later, that they had finally gone.

of course i'd want to know, says Glory. what she doesn't say: *of course i'd want to know, because she was going to leave me anyway. probably went and married that straight girl in front of city hall and God and her mother.*

k doesn't know what Glory is thinking, but she puts her hand on her shoulder and squeezes it, hoping that it means the same thing that Glory's touch feels to her. she feels Glory tighten, but she doesn't pull away like k expects her to.

Glory touches her chain (a gift from her lola), flattening it against her skin. *even if i wanted to stay with her and just not know,* she says, *that wouldn't be possible. someone would have told me. or she would have, i guess.*

k goes to the fridge and gets a bottle down from the cluster of them. she pours into her cup, and holds it up to the light, for Glory to see, raising her eyebrows. Glory shakes her head in a few small, precise movements and returns her attention to the coloring book. the cape has been abandoned. the cat's ear, enormous and spotted, is darkening, in cramped segments, each a rotation of Glory's wrist on the paper, one color at a time.

someone probably saw us, says k. *someone probably knows.*

yeah, a lot of people saw you, says Glory, shaking her head again.

we were just talking, says k. she drinks standing up.

people aren't stupid. well, they're stupid, but, says Glory, finally looking up, her glance as dark and wet as the inside of a can, *you're stupider.*

you're being really harsh, k says. she finishes the drink but the warmth hasn't gone away. she wishes she hadn't invited Glory over. she wishes Glory would leave. she wishes bea was here, but also that she won't ever have to face her.

you need someone to tell you this stuff, says Glory. *excuse me if i'm sympathizing with your girlfriend. like if this is how you treat the woman you're supposed to love most in the world, how do you think that makes the other women in your life feel?*

k creeps back to the couch. her body—tight hamstrings, aching calves—has been hurting all day. she could tell Glory that she forgot she signed up for a shift in the city tonight, go work and make some money, ride her bike all night, exhaust herself enough that she can honestly tell bea she can't see her until tomorrow.

Glory sighs. *i'm not saying your feelings don't matter, babe*, she says. *i know you're not a bad person. i'm just trying to help you see the other side, because i care about you. and bea, too.*

after Janessa, Glory didn't leave her house for days. k ended up calling her boss and telling her that Glory was having a family emergency, and found a friend, an out-of-work barista, to stand in for her so she wouldn't get fired. (*who cares about that job*, said Glory. *coffee's gonna be gone soon, anyway.*) k stayed at Glory's house, doing laundry even though Glory wouldn't change her clothes, making food that Glory wouldn't eat. k remembers trying to rub Glory's feet and Glory pulling them away. *i feel so ugly*, said Glory. *you're the prettiest girl i know*, said k, and when Glory closed her eyes again, she knew it was the wrong thing to say, and that nothing she could say would be right.

this memory makes k want to cry (*queer love is healing*), and she does. back on the couch again, she curls into the cushions, hands to eye sockets, back twisted. she doesn't want Glory to leave anymore. she wishes she could love her in practice as much as she loves her in theory (in her heart, wherever that is). she wishes Glory would put her hand back on her knee, but she doesn't.

you aren't going to tell her, are you? asks k. the cowardice burns. it's so easy to forget her friend's suffering when she thinks about what she did with the Woman in Black, and how much she regrets it. she can feel her eyes fall deeper into her head, sinking into her mouth, her lap, her gut.

of course i'm not going to, says Glory. Glory doesn't want to think of this secret as a literal burden, another thing to loosen the square of her shoulders, but she does. she remembers a discussion she once had with bea about emotional labor. at first they had seemed to agree about it, but by the end, the conversation had almost become an argument. in the background, having decided that it wasn't her place to speak, hovered k.

thank you, says k, and slowly, slowly she slides across the cushions, lowering herself to the floor, and finally, finally, Glory opens her arms and gives k the hug she's been dreading since emerging from the pantry, propping its door open so the Woman in Black could leave behind her, not looking, not telling a soul before escaping by the back gate.

MONOGAMY

it was an easy choice for bea, because she hadn't had any experience otherwise. with k, who had never done it before, it was different; exciting, even. there in the water, ceremonious as a wedding, they had made a pact with each other.

keeping it exclusive, texted Claire.

ugh. it sounds so gross when you put it like that, bea replied.

because for bea the alternative was difficult to imagine, the novelty had worn off much more quickly for her than for k. bea couldn't see herself as an old woman, or even as a middle-aged woman, who slept with people other than the person with whom she had made her home. nor could she see that person sleeping with other people. this made her feel stodgy and silly and not very queer. sometimes she thought of it as not wanting to share, which made her feel even sillier. children didn't want to share toys. dogs didn't want to share bones. she, an adult woman, was capable of sharing her someday partner with their friends and family. surely she could do it with other lovers?

but bea never forced herself to do something if she didn't feel that it was right. still, from the night she and k met, she had the paradoxical sense of approaching, but defensively. bea typically didn't see the wisdom in pursuing uncertainty, but when she did, it was with the delicacy of a person who knew it intimately, like a surgeon who, aware of the minuscule vulnerabilities of the human body, understood how strange it was that she could enter another living person and that both of them could survive the process.

bea had adapted to uncertainty by becoming an expert. she had trained herself to balance on instability like a leveler, creating an absolute on top of nothing. k hadn't been attracted to this strength at first because she hadn't known bea possessed it, but over the course of that first year, it was something she came to rely on.

THE PAST

the cancer was diagnosed a week after the beginning of sophomore year. as Mai began to get sick (her backdrop: marching band, crisping air, knee socks, weed packed into glass pipes), bea saw her friends behave in one of two ways:

some were galvanized. they threw parties around Mai's hospital bed to watch movies and talk about boys. they organized a bake sale and started an online fundraiser for her medical bills.

some were paralyzed. unable to ask what they wanted to know, they stopped texting, stopped meeting even bea's eyes in class.

the weekend after no one asked Mai to Winter Formal, Mai's mom drove the two of them to the beach. this was obviously more for Mai's mom than for Mai; before she got sick, she hadn't been at all popular. known as the weird, quiet girl who wore Dickies and ditched class to get high, she wasn't surprised or bothered that no boy, motivated by desperation or his mom's command, had shown up on her doorstep with a supermarket bouquet of flowers. *why should i care?* said Mai. but her mom insisted they take a trip anyway, and soon enough the bright, clear weather managed to take the sting off her pity. bea and Mai threw M&Ms at each other in the back seat of the van, splitting a set of headphones between them to block out the drone of talk radio.

at least Mai's mom didn't insist on tagging along with them once they got there. bea and Mai set off alone, picking up a dirt trail that disappeared into a field of ice plants. it didn't take them long to clamber down the cliffs to the water (surf: atonal wave, a musical white-noise machine, nothing at all like the app designed to mimic it).

but Mai was already tired. they sat down on a driftwood trunk, solid as granite and rooted in the sand as if it were still alive. for a long time, they looked at the ocean together without speaking. it was big enough, thought bea, that puny things like their lives and sickness and suffering could be dismissed, just not matter. it was like Mai's mom and Winter Formal and everything bad and stupid and depressing was somewhere else. here, by the water, under the sky, was a private place where posers and boys and flakes and all the other people treating Mai like she was doomed could never venture. it was just the two of them, alone together, with everything that counted spreading out ahead of them on the horizon.

then Mai broke the silence. *do they talk about me dying?* she asked. she said it so casually, as though she wanted to know if bea had time to stop for dinner on the way home, as though she didn't care what her leaving would do to the people who cared about her.

without a word, bea stood up, brushed off her jeans, and started walking back to where Mai's mom was bundled up in the driver's seat with a magazine. on the ride back home, she only spoke once, to ask Mai's mom to pull over at a gas station (hot, furious tears in the single-occupant bathroom; the coppery flavor of sink water).

by the time their friends had announced plans for a student memorial, to be held by the flagpole after school, bea and Mai hadn't spoken in months.

bea used to think regret was for isolated actions (a finger on the stove; a lie to your teacher), not movements, entire life chapters, behaviors so ingrained that they became natural law. such a misconception is why the young are able to trust so deeply in the future.

Mai's mom still emails her every once awhile, just to keep in touch. her signature has been followed by the same Bible verse, spelled out in glittery pink font, for all these years.

THE PAST

bad things happen to those who hustle, even though hustlers and hookers and pros are the best people in the world. but nothing bad—nothing *that* bad—ever happened to k when she was hustling. men had hurt her, sure, but not when she was charging.

it feels odd to have turned out safe in what was supposed to be the worst thing someone like her could do; to have been endangered just by living a certain way (*harmless little sores*) but to have made it out, relatively unscathed. to k, it often feels like she is waiting for the other shoe to drop.

LESBIAN BED DEATH

oh yeah, i forgot. Glory rolled her eyes. *dykes are supposed to be sexless. because there's no man, right? and without a man, you might as well be dead.*

but i mean it's a stereotype for a reason, right? probed k. *why would they say that if there wasn't some truth to it?*

i don't know, said Glory. *and i'm not saying it doesn't happen at all. but did you ever think about how that's something that straight people say about us?*

i guess not.

yeah. they don't know anything about like our art or our music or our culture, but somehow they know how we fuck, and how often. don't you think that's a little weird?

k had never thought about it that way before. *i guess so*, she said.

when that hit me for the first time, it got me thinking, said Glory. *that's when i realized that if straight people have something to say about us at all, they're probably wrong. in fact, the opposite of what they say is probably true. think about that for a second. think about all the things that they say about you that are lies. they say that our sex is filthy. they say that i'm in bathrooms trying to rape other women. and they say that dykes don't fuck each other. now, just what does that tell you?*

k can think of many things, and she trusts Glory implicitly, but her answer seems too easy. it makes more sense that it— everything—should be harder for queers.

THE TRAIN CAR

bea notices the shaking at the same time k sees the Woman in Black hanging from the strap opposite, headphones sculpted onto her skull, one piercing per ear, hair trailing long from beneath a snapback, shuddering as the train shudders, shaking as it shakes.

bea is too afraid to ask k if she feels it. she is afraid of what it could mean if k also feels it. this shaking is so much greater than the normal kind you expect on the train that it could only be an earthquake, or the beginnings of one.

bea does not know if an earthquake would be more severe underground or if they would be safer here, perhaps trapped for a long time, forced to take the escape route detailed on the wall of every car, jostling and pushing or queuing up with collected calm, abandoning bicycles and strollers, linking hands with k to pull the woman from out of her wheelchair and carry her down the long, echoing chamber, all the way back to the Oakland shipping yard where the tube opens from the earth, not in a natural maw or a smoking medieval gash but with a tidy, industrial anus.

unless the tracks were obstructed, and then they would never escape. they would be safe but dead, insulated from the falling concrete, spontaneous combustion, careening motor vehicles, the inexplicable puncture and flood of the Embarcadero station, which would sink like a ship even deeper into the earth. dying together sounds romantic, until you actually begin to wonder if you would claw your partner, if your lungs would fight hers for air, if you could stand to hear her weep or scream while you did the same, your end together not a bed but a live burial.

bea is trying to get a grip. there was nothing in the Seismic Update this morning, or the news (NEW FEDERAL BUDGET TO INCLUDE FUNDS FOR WORLD'S LARGEST MIGRANT DETENTION CENTER—). *everything is fine*, bea thinks, but she checks her phone again. for a moment she has service, then a paid ad dips down— BLACK FRIDAY QUAKEPREP SALE. PEACE OF MIND FOR THE HOLIDAYS!—before her connection finally disappears.

at second glance, now k isn't sure if it is her. the (possible) Woman in Black holds her phone in front of her, as if preparing to look at it, but she's gazing straight ahead. it's unclear if she is examining her reflection in the black window behind k and bea, or staring frankly at them. *is it her?* k wonders, but she can't know for sure without moving and risking drawing attention to herself. one half of the woman's face is visible, obscuring the other half from where k is standing, her arm around bea's waist. a strange guilt, shame for wearing a shirt that betrays the fact of her tits (no binder today), lights on her, weighing down deep into her sternum.

together, bea and k are afraid, separately unaware that the other is upset, and terrified that she will notice her own fear. *are you okay?* someone should have asked, one or the other. *are you alright, baby?* but neither did.

bea grips k's hand where it landed on her hip, panic's precise, intractable lens making her vision crisp. oscillating before it like the guts of a men's electric razor is a scattered recall of statistics, data, news reports, clicks, wikis, op-eds, notions and concepts and theories. bea rarely takes the train, whereas k takes it almost every day, sees the same TSA agents and hears the same announcements and reads the same ads (HELP US RENAME THE GREAT PACIFIC GARBAGE PATCH & GET SIX MONTHS OF QUADRANT 1 ISLAND HOUSING FREE!), and she does not seem afraid, seems completely calm, but then again k is always calm, or so it seems to bea. the last train bea took—the one that brought them into the city this afternoon, where there was a horror movie they both liked playing on a wall in a dive bar that served free popcorn sprinkled with nutritional yeast—had been safe. bea hadn't even had to close her eyes and count to ten, over and over again, to survive the five minutes between West Oakland and Embarcadero, even though she'd felt a little unsettled this morning when she was getting ready: keys lost, out of cereal, a few small work obligations shifting around behind her eyes, the kind of things that should have made her mind wander back over to the black field where she is spending more and more of her time (IN TAIPEI,

HUNDREDS JUMP FROM BUILDINGS DURING FIRE CAUSED BY QUAKE), the crowded cell of worry, anticipating and wondering.

but then they met on the platform and k smiled at her, her backpack full of whiskey and trail mix and cigarettes, ready to go somewhere together—it didn't matter where. k's black hair, her smile, her long, straight build. no one jostled them as they got onto the train, and from the first moment they set foot on the peninsula bea hadn't even thought of the Big One, not until after the movie, anyway, when she should have been sleepy and happy and ready to be home in bed, drifting off with k.

k's heart beats hot inside her, loose and fragile as a yolk. she resists the urge to let go of bea's hand and step away from her body, to wrap her arms around herself, hold herself together on this dim and rocking train. she pretends that the woman on the strap across from them isn't the woman from the pantry, even though she doesn't know for sure either way. she hopes that bea won't see her and know, hopes that if the woman *is* the Woman in Black that she will see k with bea and understand and leave her alone. *see me with her, see me happy. please see me and stop seeing me. please.*

and k is happy, or was, the warmth of bea's warmth— leather jacket, brief braids, broad honey smile—taking up all of the space that k needs full to feel safe. safe all day, her arm around bea in the Mission, bea's hand on her knee in the movie, sharing the flask until it was empty. what movie had they gone to see? k remembers it now, but in a week, a year, a hundred years from now, will she remember that today they went to the city to walk and look and watch that movie? perhaps. but if she doesn't, if all that falls away, even the memory, there will still be k and bea, bea's warmth so radiant there were even a few moments today when k forgot about what she'd done, and what she has to do.

it goes without saying that she has not told bea what happened. the ache of this secret is only eclipsed by her fury with herself. the woman on the train today is in all likelihood just another Bay Area queer, but what's the difference between a memory and a ghost? k hasn't seen the Woman in Black since that night in the pantry. no one aside from Glory has mentioned her to k. photos from that evening show everyone else—Ken, Arianna, Glory's friends—but not her, and not even the algorithms of k's social media had drudged her up for friendship or following. and of course, Glory kept her promise—she hasn't told anyone, least of all bea.

until today, the Woman in Black could have evaporated, could have never existed, could have been a test sent by a strange but no less wrathful god (and failure was inevitable, because who defeats god, much less themselves?). and then this woman on the train, who could be the Woman in Black, but a tall collar, a shower of hair, and bea, slightly in the way, prevent k from knowing for sure. is it her, or someone else with an attractive, showy mouth and the flat, masculine physique k desires, aesthetically and, it seems, in other ways, too? bea's face is only available in contrast: a study in guilt.

if k were outside of the train car, instead of inside it, with only her girlfriend standing between her and that woman, if she were somewhere else—on the platform, overlooking the ocean, at the edge of a bridge—she would jump, off or in.

but bea is right beside her, and k can't look at her face. she imagines it instead. bea's smile, bea's tears, bea asleep, silent but moveable (the sore), her countenance like water behind a pane of glass: light and shade—hair, lip, eyelid, throat—that come together like autumn here, or spring somewhere else. her arm around k's waist, bea stands beside her, trusting, idle, thinking pure things, or loving things, or planning, as bea likes to do, or perhaps thinking of nothing at all (which is what k likes best, cresting Russian Hill after the climb, heaving herself up onto the top of her own little mountain and falling into the gravity on the other side), residing in the peace due her (coffee-brown eyes that only a few minutes before marbled under the sunshine slatting, glaring, pouring into the moving windows). white teeth and white whites of the eye, bea: always smelling, even in this pissful train car, even under k's sinful arm, even between her and the maybe-person k fucked in a dark and public place, like citron and crushed rose petals and healthy perspiration (she likes walking in the nighttime down old distinguished streets and uprooting succulents from the manicured yards. she brings them home and plants them in her own ceramic and plastic tubs, an almost-shattered toilet tank under the window).

if god—the testing god that hates queers but hates deceit even more—if he would let the Woman in Black (*is it her? it is. it's not!*) continue to stare ahead, absorbed in her headphones, flexing her knees against the hurtling momentum of the train, perhaps dreaming about her own girl, or more than one girl, a girl or girls that she loves as much as k loves bea, let her go on unlooking at them and leave them alone, and not turn to k, and speak to her, and force her to reveal herself to bea (because k knows that if the Woman in Black speaks to her, even if all she says is *hi*, the truth will appear on her face as legibly as the tattoos on her arms), if god will only be so merciful, then k will do the thing she has been imagining (penance) and never tell bea a word (grace). she will worry about penance for her penance later, penance for that and for, unbelievably, the excitement she feels, knowing how close she is to complete unhappiness *(if bea leaves me),* that darkness its own promise of relief.

THE SORE

if she could have grown her own sore on her lower lip (its favorite perch three times a year like clockwork, when she's outside too much in the rain or surviving off caffeine pills), k could give it to herself. that was the first solution, the easiest one, if not the most satisfying.

autofellatio is unnecessary. all you have to do is swab the carbuncle—Q-tip or finger, like medicine, or makeup, primer, foundation, concealer—and rub the target mucous membrane, thorough, ungentle, to spread the virus into fresh cells. infection is so easy, she doesn't even remember how it happened in the first place. (her aunt said: *you were born with it.*)

lack of sleep has, in the past, caused outbreaks, and for a while after bea's sore, k waited expectantly, her insomnia tempered by the certainty of its appearance. but the weeks went by and nothing happened. awake next to bea, or at her own house, lying on her bed or posted up on the futon if her roommate was out, she rubbed her lower lip with the fat cushion of her index finger, feeling, somehow, that a persistent pressure, a subtle irritant, might somehow encourage one to grow.

it didn't. turns out the secret to beating the virus is, as it is for every one of life's obstacles, embracing it, racing after it, pining and losing sleep for it. what k wants, k can't have. and so now that she has made this promise to god (penance, grace, etc.), there is nothing else to do but outsource her infection.

GOING OFFLINE

the apartment is in an old building with a lobby that plays ten-year-old pop music through a hidden speaker. the elevator is narrow and slow, the kind you watch through a porthole as it descends to the ground floor. once the light has filled the little window from top to bottom, you have to open it yourself with the cold metal handle

k wants to take the stairs, but her stomach hurts and she is going up really high. the possibility of vomiting, or of needing to pull down her pants in the elevator and shit on the floor, hoping desperately that she can get off and away before anyone else gets on, doesn't come and go: it is in residence (she refuses to consider how the rest of the fantasy would play out on the train back to where her bike is locked, the long, cold ride home from the station). still, she waits for the car to hit the ground floor. when the porthole lights up, she gets in.

k gets in elevators all the time for her job. someone taps on their phone and she picks up baggies of hot food, compostable cartons of pad thai, bottles of beer, jars of bud, bouquets of flowers, sealed envelopes full of papers, and then she brings it to that someone. the delivery part's not so bad, and she's fast. the hard part is getting the ordered items from the street up to the homes of the people who order it.

first, k waits for the person behind the desk to open the sliding front door (a woman walks through the lobby, a wheezing purebred in a golden sweater under her arm). then she waits for the doorperson to call up and confirm that k's order actually exists (a man walks through the lobby, $500 headphones crowning the $100 fade he could have gotten in the hood for half the price). then the doorperson escorts her to an elevator and pushes a button, which won't activate until they swipe an ID card. sometimes the doorperson even accompanies her on the elevator, adjusting their cufflinks, smoothing their hair, avoiding k with their eyes or smiling vacantly, the silent *shoom* of the car rising up ten, twenty, a hundred floors—maybe higher—the stainless steel box reeking of lavender antibacterial fair trade free-range detergent. when they get to the correct floor, the doorperson leads her through the labyrinth (is there another word for spaces that are intentionally confusing, or at least intentionally anonymous? like who designed this place? who is responsible for it? do the people who live here truly never get lost? what's with the alcoves in the wall, like those altars you can still find in older buildings, but that are filled with sterile electric lights, or single orchids in glass bottles that immigrant workers come to replace every other day?), to the apartment with the very small bell and very small welcome mat, watching as she rings and the customer answers: a young white man in a bathrobe signing for a bag of grapes, deli meats, XL condoms. a young Asian man, a stack of free weights a few feet from the door, signing for a takeaway burger with a side of macaroni and cheese. a poreless, middle-aged woman with a Korean surname who signs for a pack of Parliaments and an expensive bottle of wine. a poreless, middle-aged woman with a German surname with bruises under her eyes and perfectly symmetrical bandages on her nose who signs for salad nicoise with seared tuna. the countless young women of all races and sizes who take the triple pint of ice cream, box of sausage pizza, foot-long ham and cheese sub, tray of double-chocolate cookies as fast as they can, their panic and furious joy enough to push k back a few inches while they fuss with the plastic and rush the door closed, never looking at her face.

though it took a while, k feels like she now understands these big buildings, these apartments and condos, better than most. when she started her job, she couldn't believe so many people lived in towers with better security than any business she'd stolen from or theme park she'd broken into, with cameras in every corner, where nothing could be opened or closed without swiping some object (key, fob, card) embedded with intelligence. she's used to it now.

the fluorescent buttons protrude from the wall and are hard to push in all the way, but after a moment, the car begins to move. it is so slow, she takes her phone from her pocket and scrolls through Twitter for a moment (LONG READ: HOW POLICE BECAME THE MOST PROTECTED CLASS) before double-checking to make sure her notifications are still on, the volume on her phone all the way up.

you want me to call you at 9? asked Glory. her voice sounded strange, almost unfamiliar, over the phone.

yeah and if i don't pick up, keep calling until i do, said k. her voice felt strange coming out of her mouth.

your alarm broke or something? what are you doing tonight?

k had considered coming up with a lie, but eventually decided against it. she couldn't think of one that was actually believable (*i'm hustling again and need someone to check in—i'm getting dinner with my shitty Evangelical cousin and need a fake emergency—*), but she knows if she needs Glory not to know, Glory will understand.

i can't tell you. i'm sorry. but it's important.

okay. said Glory. her silence could have been hesitation, judgment, pity, nothing. *okay, honey.*

thank you, k said. at that moment fear surged through her, and she grasped for something, for the idea of bea (white split; red-hot tail), but she couldn't picture her clearly. would she ever tell Glory about all this, all of what had happened with bea, and all of what she felt she had to do? somehow, it felt more possible than telling bea, and of course, bea could never know.

how about this. Glory's voice was soft, much softer than it usually was. the strong, clear mezzo-soprano of someone who spends her time behind a counter had dimmed like a firefly. *how about you send me an address. for my peace of mind. don't have to tell me why.*

there were so many big things, so many permanences to wade through that even consequences had become details. it was all too much for one person to understand, to do on their own. *you never ask anyone for help.* Glory had said this before, with the best of intentions. *i have to force it on you.*

but Glory didn't understand that the risk was not in the needing, but in the asking, because if you asked, it was possible that your request would be denied.

i'll text it to you, said k. when they hung up, she sat looking at her phone, the screen (OP-ED: DRONE-WARFARE TECHNOLOGY MUST ADAPT TO CLIMATE CHANGE, JUST LIKE THE REST OF US) still bright and colorful as a pinball machine.

THE BIG ONE

are you headed to the meeting?

Lita's voice startles bea into a jump. by instinct, the fingers
of her left hand open an empty tab. she doesn't know if Lita
saw what she was watching. would she care? probably not.
but bea still wants to keep her secret from everyone (though
from k most of all).

when it comes to k, bea's secrets vary in degree and
management. some of them she conceals intentionally—like
the fact that she doesn't like bicycling all *that* much—but
others are secret by happenstance, like the things that she
knows solely by virtue of her own experience. for instance,
bea is older than k, which might be why she understands
that there is a difference between sensitivity and empathy,
while k does not.

for example: knowing one's partner is sad, or lonely, or
anxious is no simple matter of knowing, of an awareness
based on electricity and subconscious metaphysical
vibrations and long, loving proximity; nor is this awareness
worth anything if it can't also be internalized.

yeah, i'll be there, says bea. *just finishing this up and i'll head over.* another video is loading by the time Lita turns the corner. while she waits, the thoughts that she had been trying to avoid returned, clamoring for attention: k is not sleeping. k does not want to have sex. using a variety of excuses, k is withdrawing from her more and more, is seeing less of her, and even of Glory, than she has ever since they met.

and yet, when they are together, there is something in k—a deep needfulness, her eyes shimmering like tears—that bea can feel, palpable as the mouse in her right hand. k touches bea less than she did before, but when bea touches her, k folds into bea's body (timed release: a tropical flower opening in the twilight) before stirring, as if in recognition, and retreating back to wherever her mind is these days.

if bea confessed everything to her mom or Claire or a therapist or an advice columnist, all would confirm that bea is in denial about k and their future together, a denial that she is allowing to grow stronger with every passing day. and perhaps they would be right. bea knows this is something she should talk about with k (*honesty*), and she looks at her phone, sitting beside her keyboard. but then the screen catches her attention again, and she opens another tab, then another, then returns to the original video, the one that's still loading, looking to scratch that itch, eyes widening in the glow of her screen, the scrolling numbers, the slideshows, the threads of diagrams and propositions.

and then her alarm goes off, and it's time for her meeting. the video she wanted is still loading. with a sigh, bea closes the window.

THE SORE

k has always thought that people place too much stock in dreams. it wasn't just woo people like bea who were deluded enough to trust their lives to the neurological equivalent of a fart.

like a self-cleaning stove, one's brain (the hot upper floor) gives itself an automatic going-over whenever one sleeps (the firmament boiling itself clean). or else it goes to work with all the humanity of a bot, assembling a puzzle from desires and anxieties and fears styled in the archetypes of one's own culture, fitting together their interchangeable parts and then shooting the amalgam to your inbox. when people thought dreams meant things, concrete things, k wanted to roll her eyes. what does a change in your blood pressure mean, on a psychological level? one might as well psychoanalyze a dump.

after two sleepless nights in a row, she white-knuckles her bike up three flights of stairs at Montgomery Station. the aura of warm piss has the body of perfume. she only worked four hours today, the breakdown miserable, the tips worse. when she gets home, she turns off her phone, draws the curtains, and lies down over her blankets, the stink of her labor just starting to materialize under her arms and between her thighs.

an hour later, a dream awakens her. she can't remember this ever happening to her before, a dream actually hardening into real life, flying into her face like a white bird. she sits up, rubbing her eyes, her dried perspiration alive again, and melting.

the content the dream: k's body outstretched and transparent, Vitruvian, Mendietan, empty as a hot-water bottle, legs spread. a hand (*whose?*) lifts a lit match up through the thighs, and now the inside is illuminated like a cave without a wall painting. it's empty, no rot to be seen, but nothing that grows, either.

blinking, k's hand flies to her lip, hopeful for a moment. she turns her phone back on herself and takes the photo that confirms it: still nothing, still no sore of her own. a text buzzes through from a number she hasn't saved but recognizes nevertheless:

8 works for me. see you tonight.

THE BIG ONE

what are you most afraid of in the world? asks bea.

Claire answers easily, like she was waiting for this question. *is it stupid to say that i'm afraid of Nick dying?* she asks.

why would that be stupid? asks bea, though she does think it's stupid.

because he's my boyfriend. he's not like my mom or anything. Claire passes bea the joint, picks up the disposable camera, and straightens the sheet beneath them. the afternoon isn't quite warm enough for a picnic, but bea brought a blanket for them to share. Claire points the camera at her.

i don't think it's stupid, says bea. *but that's because i feel the same way.*

about Nick? Claire laughs.

bea laughs, too. *you know i mean k*, she says. her laugh becomes a cough, and Claire leans over to pat her back, still laughing.

on the trail that wraps around the Lake, people in spandex and sweatshirts are running and walking and cycling and pushing strollers and talking into headphones. a herd of geese, black heads bobbing like needles (a fleet of sewing machines), waddles toward the eastern side of the park. bea admires their wings. they can leap into flight at any sign of danger, vault into the air and head straight for Canada, where there is socialized health care and poutine. bea imagines them taking off mere moments before the Big One (RISK OF SUPERQUAKE ON WEST COAST "A MEDIA DISTRACTION," POTUS SAYS), pointing their beaks north, their shadows stark against the crumbling Oakland skyline bearing down on itself as it rolls downward—30, 40, 50 stories vibrating, shuddering, shivering, a meniscus on the verge of breaking (an insect on the water) on the largest imaginable scale, like multiple 9/11s—and into the earth.

to be honest, says bea, *i think i'm actually more scared of something else.*

Claire is still pointing the camera at bea. beneath the lens, her smile pauses. *what is it?* she asks. she is listening, but part of her attention, the small but persistent fraction of her awareness that dwells in the memory and certainty of a particular potential future, remains targeted on Nick in death, on the strength of this possibility (women live longer than men, because women are stronger, women endure) of an elderly life, or even a mature life, without him, alone, no children, awaiting the death of her friends (*queer love is healing*) and the degradation of her own body. at what age is one too advanced to find another love, another comfort, another body to be close with? what will happen to her, alone, dependent on others, at 75, at 80, good for another few years, perhaps more, without him, too tired, too infirm, too much in pain, the day-to-day of arthritis and still worsening, anticipating her end? Claire thinks of her grandmother: court TV in a recliner, weeping behind the screen door when she and her dad have to go home again.

it seems stupid to admit, after a fear as momentous as the death of a loved one, that bea is afraid of mere death itself. but the Big One isn't exactly death, is it? careful bea, precise bea, doesn't know how to articulate to her friend the fear of an uncontrolled demise, the fear of an unknown moment, the future an uncertain certainty, of not knowing how to live with the anticipation.

i'm afraid of natural disasters, i guess. bea tucks the blanket under her legs. she tries to sound like she's joking.

that makes sense, says Claire. the camera clicks.

that's not really it though, bea rushes to say. *it's earthquakes, specifically.*

i've heard those are pretty bad around here, says Claire, laughing. she moved to San Francisco from Nebraska with her first boyfriend six years ago. they didn't make it in the city long. suffocated by the buildings, Trent moved on to Dallas to strike it rich in the Deregulated Zone, where he only had to confront the skyscrapers when he wasn't at work on an oil rig. defeated by the rent, Claire did what thousands of white transplants before her had done and moved to Oakland.

bea often forgets that her fear is not legible to everyone who knows her, even though she doesn't talk about it with anyone, not even k, who knows about it only superficially (once: an especially drunk evening at home, bea showed k some of her favorite earthquake videos, studying her face for her reaction, disappointed, almost angered, by the apathy she saw there). she has never even said it aloud: *i am afraid of the Big One.* it's a fear that everyone talks about all the time (THE QUESTION ISN'T WHEN, IT'S HOW BIG), has been in the air for years, but bea can't speak its name, not even to k.

did you know, says bea, *that the likelihood of a really big earthquake happening in the next two years is more than eighty percent?*

no, says Claire. she holds the camera in her two hands like sandwich. *i didn't. or maybe i did. i guess it's not something i worry about. you get kind of desensitized. it seems like they're always saying that.*

i think about leaving a lot, admits bea. *i mean, it's not like i should be here anyway, gentrifying.*

you would leave? because of the earthquake? where would you go?

i don't know, says bea. she doesn't know why she's still here. it suddenly seems insane to have not packed up and gone inland years ago.

other places have other kinds of natural disasters, Claire observes.

well, i know that, admits bea. she feels her throat thickening.

she's getting upset, but doesn't know why. *i know that. but this one is going to destroy everything. it doesn't matter what we do.*

would you really leave, bea? the fraction of Claire that remembers, in advance (embroidered on a pillow: "Worrying is like praying for something you don't want to happen"; previous nightmares), Nick's death has perked up, is stretching outwards, flexing in front of the mirror. all of her friends leaving her alone, even in the future, in the anti-history. no one will be around for her to call, to sit with in the sun, to pose for her photos. no one. Nick dead. alone without him in a small living room.

bea checks her phone. she started this conversation with Claire because she wanted to talk about k, but didn't know how, and it's gone in a completely different direction. she wants to talk about how she is afraid of k's fear, afraid of k's sadness. she wants to talk about the thing that has come between them, and her suspicion that it is irreconcilable. she wants to talk about her certainty that if she and k talk about it, they will summon into being that particular ghost, and then she really will have to leave, forever (*alone*), because the threat of the Big One is already almost more than she can bear.

i really don't know, says bea. she checks her phone again. if she left, would k come with her?

when bea gets home a few hours later, she calls her mom. she buys a train ticket. she texts her boss. she packs a duffel with clothes, her makeup, a book. she knocks on her roommate's door and talks with her for a few minutes.

when everything is ready—her bag by the welcome mat, her cat provided for, her boss informed, and her plants (four little cacti in clay pots, a gardenia she hasn't yet transplanted from its forest-green plastic cup, the bromeliad in its ceramic) watered—she texts k.

THE BIG ONE

back when the tremors began, when Seismic Updates were still the first thing you checked on your phone when you woke up, people knew they were afraid. things were changing in an obvious way, and everyone knew it was only going to get worse, so they got ready. they collected canned food and hosted geological teach-ins. to take the edge off waiting, they held End of the Bay–themed dance parties (cover charge going toward retrofitting the nearest homeless shelter) and talked self-indulgently about which survival skills they could offer after the apocalypse.

but as time passed and the tremors became more frequent (every day and every night, interrupted by a few larger quakes), the Big One still didn't materialize. from on high—scientists, the government, the media—came warnings and reassurances, promises and threats made and then immediately broken and rendered null and void, or at least forgotten with the next cycle of environmental terror and political outrage. the push and pull mediated the long, arduous burn of expectation, of the real news and the fake news and the rumors and the guesswork, and somehow the

Big One became background noise, something taxonomized and hashtagged but leeched of meaning, a possibility deprived of its potential.

k can't remember if bea was afraid of earthquakes when they met, but she knows that she's afraid of them now, and it seems as if it's getting worse. she understands irrational fear, so she doesn't think it's useful to tell bea not to practice hers. but in the time since they met, bea's has grown from a preoccupation to a fixation, has gotten so big that even k, sleepless and frenzied, with a great big, impending terror of her own, has noticed it.

once, a few weeks after the sore: they were sitting in bea's kitchen on their laptops. k heard a noise, and looked up to see bea crying.

are you okay? said k. *what are you watching?*

she stood up and went around to bea's side of the table. on the screen was a video so still it could have been a photo. the only thing moving on the beautiful sunlit beach was the waves, gently lapping the sand without a sound. the title of the video—TSUNAMI (WAIT FOR IT)—was obscured below the toolbar.

what is this? said k.

nothing, said bea. her eyes were trained on the screen, on the beautiful place where nothing was happening. *i think i'm just PMSing.*

k went back to her own laptop and didn't say anything else, but she spent her next sleepless night regretting it.

THE SORE

he is white. he is older but not old. not attractive but not ugly, either. under the light above the front door, k sees that his cheekbones and the pads of his fingers are pink. he is wearing a polo and slacks. no wedding band. a pile of junk mail on the table by the door. he leads her inside.

would you like a drink? he asks.

it is dim in the apartment. the only light comes from above the stove and from a lamp behind the couch. the kitchen is neat, and nothing of its components—utensils, cereal boxes, washcloths—are to be seen. has he cleaned because k is coming, or is it always this immaculate? and which is more despicable?

okay, k says. he moves over to the cabinet, opens it, and pulls out two short glasses.

k is always aware of her body, but she learned a long time ago that this is not typical of men who everyone agrees are men. unfortunately, it's during those rare times that she loses sight of it, when her body falls away (pure focus or pure pain), that she needs that awareness the most. at work on her bike, wrenching her handlebars through Market Street traffic, screwed into precarious balance between a paused bus (KEEP AMERICA SAFE. JOIN ICE.) and a changing light, flying down Steiner or Pacific or Columbia, she should be knowing her body, but can't. freedom is dangerous.

the man hands her the glass and she drinks without asking what it is. how is she knowing her body now? she assesses: it is difficult to close her lips over her mouth and keep them there, because she's congested. her glutes are sore, as are the joints of her hands. her pants feel too tight across her thighs, as does her skin across her body. she puts the cup to her mouth, and the ice cools the frayed skin of her lips. as she drinks, the sound of the gulping inside her head expands. she feels herself expanding (a balloon filling with the breath of a dying woman).

she is afraid she won't go through with it. she is afraid she'll change her mind and he'll rape her. she is afraid that she will do this and bea will find out and hate her. she is afraid she will do this and it won't change anything.

did you have any trouble finding it? he asks politely. he is tall and soft, not generous but fleshy, his pants fitting neatly, his socks perfectly matched. the pleat of his khakis around his crotch is too ample, almost obscenely so. k doesn't want to see what is beneath them, but she might have to anyway: it is too dim to see his mouth, and so she does not know for sure where his sore could be. even if it's on his mouth, later on he might undo his pants, slyly, and put it in her hand, acting surprised when she pushes it away, pretending not to know that all she wants is transmission.

no, says k.

good, he says. *i'm glad you came. i wasn't sure you would.*

you just move? k says. there are no photos or posters on the walls. other than the couch, there is no furniture in the living room, although the kitchen seems well stocked.

he smiles, subtly thrusting his khaki toward her, inching across the floor on his socks. *actually,* he says, *i'm borrowing it from a friend. i live in the South Bay.*

did your friend just move? k asks. she doesn't know why. she doesn't care who lives here.

he laughs, inching a little closer. *i don't know. i haven't known him very long.*

SWITCHING

i think i want to stop, k said.

oh, said bea. *okay. that's okay.* she remembers pulling away. (in k's memory, she recoiled.)

i don't want to make you do anything you don't want to, k said.

of course i want to, of course! cried bea. she was kneeling, helpless, the cock jutting out before her, her shoulders slumped like an unwatered plant. *of course! i'm sorry. did i do something? i'm sorry!* she swiftly flipped onto her back, struggling to pull off the harness so she could take k in her arms.

i think i just want to go to sleep, k said. she rolled over and away from bea. her shoulders collapsed inward, her body shrinking smaller and smaller. bea remembers staying in her own cold corner of k's bed until the next morning. k recalls sleeping alone.

both bea and k still have a few memories from that time, but what happened, remains happened? both have preserved it differently, and yet it must have happened in a particular way. how can that be? who is right? this aperture persists, still bridging a before and an after that they share, a mystery that is as real as another memory, one forgotten by both but which will always exist:

in the blue sheet, worn, clean but stained by pomegranate juice and menstrual blood, under her body, their bodies, brown and pink, a rolling, an angle, a face: quantity unthought, softness, bruises like clouding tea. leave a mark or not. sucking the thin skin of her ribs and leaving long stains of clotted blood, subdermal, swelling a shade darker. a rare sweet time of making each other, technicality and expertise and intent gone. bite marks building new erogenous zones. tears, because we are fluid-bound.

GONE

bea's hometown is a few hours north and east of the Bay, far beyond the subduction zone, safe in the sunburnt hills. she's wanted to get a car for years, but the money never seems to materialize. a last-minute ticket wasn't too expensive, but the trip is taking much longer than usual because there is a delay at the Sacramento station. they were scheduled to leave an hour ago, but a Seismic Update put a hold on all departures from her terminal.

passengers roam the aisles, heading downstairs to the snack bar or hunting the shortest bathroom line. bea stays in her seat, scrolling through the updates. she can't find anything nearby. maybe the Amtrak people are just blaming a run-of-the-mill delay on a made-up tremor. she refreshes and looks again.

k still hasn't texted back. (unseen by bea, a flock of birds whorls in from the fading sunlight and darts upward, disappearing into the eaves of the terminal.) bea takes deep breaths, anchors herself in her seat, her feet flat against the floor, but calm is a finite resource, and hers is tapped. she was calm as she talked to her mom on the phone, calm as she texted her boss and told her she was taking off the rest of the week for a family emergency. she was calm as she unzipped the rolling suitcase and put her clothes inside: some shirts, a pair of pants, and a skirt because it will be warmer in the valley, though she brought stockings, too. she was calm as she packed too many pairs of clean panties (her habit when she travels) and her toothbrush and her Diva cup, calm when she changed the litter box and put out the bag of kibble where her roommate could find it.

if silence and slow movements are what calm is, then she is calm. but water condenses along her forehead and scores the bones of her spine.

i'm going to my mom's for awhile. bea had sent the text on the sidewalk in front of her apartment. i took off work.

what's wrong?? k's response had taken a few minutes, enough time for a garbage truck to make its way as far as 34th Street. bea replied immediately.

all this waiting is getting to me. it's driving me crazy.

what are you talking about? but k realized what bea meant as soon as she sent the text. bea confirmed it with swift brutality:

i just can't be here when it happens.

bea didn't send another text asking k to come with her, but then again, k didn't reply.

what does bea know? only what k told her, which was that k can't stand to see her, because k is too fucked up. k didn't tell her this with her words. she told her with her body, has been telling her ever since the sore.

this morning, bea woke up and turned her head to where k always sleeps, and there she was, her lids wide and red-rimmed, her mouth sagging open, a crumbling powder gathered at the corners of the eyes that glared into her phone.

had she been up all night again? when was the last time bea had seen k asleep? when was the last time bea had known k to sleep? she left to meet up with Claire (today was a precious day off that they had together) and while she hadn't yet made a decision, the one germinating inside her was insistent enough that she thought to grab her spare toothbrush from k's bathroom.

again unseen, the birds suddenly reappear, disturbed for some unknowable reason from their nightly nesting, before vanishing back into the twilight, a scattered mob. the screen on bea's phone changes. someone is calling her.

THE SORE

k finishes her second drink. *so*, she says, *where is it?*

he smiles like a doll. the rim of his glass is crystal-clear, untouched by his lips. *i'm sorry?* he says politely.

k sighs. *come on*, she says. *is it on your mouth?*

his face moves toward her slightly. in this lighting, it's still difficult to see it very well. though she'd rather not take her eyes off him, k checks her phone again, though she would have heard if Glory called. the screen is black. Glory hasn't called, of course; it's still too early.

where do you want me to have it? he laughs. his face retreats back into shadow. *don't worry*, he goes on. stretching out his hand, he touches her shoulder. *we've got time.*

k doesn't mirror him with her own smiles or laughter—she's not working. her face remains blank, baiting the silence. his grin weakens, then goes slack, curdling to something slightly less happy than before.

let's just talk for a while first. he seems just a little exasperated now, his lips (pink fault line) struggling to recover. *we don't have to rush.*

okay, says k. she checks her phone again. bea must be at her mom's by now, but she hasn't texted her since this afternoon. k wishes she would. k wishes she could be anywhere else but here, but even more, she wishes she was with bea.

why don't we get comfortable? he says.

the couch is softly suede. they sit side by side, like friends. there's no coffee table, so k sets her empty glass on the carpet. she's not worried about it falling over. something she's learned from delivering in the skyscrapers of San Francisco: you don't feel tremors this high up, not the same way you feel them when you're on the ground.

how do you feel? he says. he seems relaxed again.

fine, says k. she makes it a point to look around, as if taking in the details. her arm is stiff, to dissuade him from brushing up against it with his.

i feel pretty good, he offers. he puts his drink on the carpet, too. the couch creaks as he leans toward her. it's still too dim to see.

so, says k, *where are your medical records?* she pulls back a little as she says it, hoping the question will distract him.

what? nothing about his voice or his face, that she can see anyway, indicates true curiosity. all that there is is the word. why doesn't he even bother to conceal his desire to lie?

your medical records, says k. *remember? i asked for them.*

oh. yes. he says it as if he had forgotten what brought them together this evening. he gets to his feet and goes back into the kitchen. k hears a drawer rolling, the tapping of something on the countertop. would she know if they were fake? she thinks she would.

um, he says. there are more sounds, more drawers. *actually, i don't know if it's here.*

it's not on your phone? says k.

it's here somewhere.

k doesn't know what to do. should she just leave, without getting what she came for? she thought of all the time-wasters to arrive on time at their motel rooms only to try to shortchange her, and the righteous fury she took in leaving them with their hard-ons (less pleasant to recall were the times she needed the money and stayed). but while cash is negotiable, infection is not, especially when it could come with more than she bargained for, and she won't do that, she won't risk bea (*bea's body*) again. the only way to be absolutely sure she doesn't do that is to go home, where there is nothing, not even the satisfaction (penance) she wants so desperately. home, where only the horrifying prospect of doing this all over again—sleepless, furious, frightened, broke—awaits her. nothing good is there at home, not even Glory or Ken or even her roommate (visiting family in Florida). certainly not bea.

bea. k wonders where she is. probably at home with her mom, unless she's drinking at her hometown's only gay bar, purring in a group of newfound femmes, people who haven't known her long enough to fail her like k has. she wonders whether bea will text her again. with a lurch that revives the pain in her stomach, she wishes she had replied (i just can't be here when it happens.), had promised to come find her. and she would have, if she hadn't needed to be here—wouldn't she?

and she does need to be here. all of this can't be for nothing, all of this can't add up to yet another mistake—abandoning bea in her fear—when the ultimate outcome is going to save her.

why don't you just show it to me, says k. she should know what it (*bea's body*) looks like by now.

okay. his voice sounds relieved. he comes back from the kitchen and sinks into the couch with a sigh. *but*, he goes on, *i would like to know why you want it.*

k is surprised. *why?*

don't you think it matters? from the depths of his comfort, he tilts his head, his hands spread wide open like a punchline.

he laughs, a fruity, manufactured noise. *why are we even here if it doesn't matter?*

it sounds so absurd. *why are we even here if it doesn't matter?* the phrase could be on a poster, or a bumper sticker. k's curiosity dissipates. he just wants an excuse to talk to her, to leech out of her as much as he possibly can. she hadn't anticipated this, and that was stupid of her. men never want just your body—they want everything else, too.

THE PAST

some fucking man touched me today. bea said it casually, like she was commenting on today's tremor.

what happened? said k. she decided the best way to stay calm was to keep looking at her food. if bea wasn't upset, she shouldn't be either.

i don't know, bea said, shrugging. *just another man who felt like he needed to grab my ass.* she spooned in another mouthful.

k was shocked. *really? what did you do?* she forgot to look at her food. *did you get in his face?* this is what she would have done.

of course not, said bea. *of course i didn't.*

why not?

because that's stupid.

it's not stupid. now k felt stupid for suggesting it. she tried to explain herself. *you need to stand up to those guys. shame them publicly.* k was used to bad attention from men; she understood that they looked for victims. her way of surviving wasn't stupid, not if it had worked.

well, that's not how i handle it, bea said. she sniffed.

well, maybe you should. now k was angry.

i don't want to talk about it anymore. forget about it.

k (afraid she would crack open) didn't want to talk about it anymore, either. but she wanted bea to understand her, to see that she was trying to help. it seemed unfair that there were a million ways to be wrong, and only one to be right. she made another attempt.

i just worry about you, bea, she said. *i hate it when that shit happens to you.*

yeah, said bea. she wouldn't look at her. *me too.* k realized, with a shock, that she was on the verge of tears.

they didn't talk for a long time, and their evening continued on, the space of time between dinner and bea's bed long and bleak, like a crowded beach on a hot, cloudless day. but when they finally got under the blankets, k's arms around bea, their legs tangled up in the warm and soft-cornered space, their conversation continued.

i'm sorry, said k. she was still angry.

it's not my fault that shit happens, bea replied. she was also still angry.

i know. i'm sorry. she felt other things through her anger, alongside it, and she brought her body closer to bea's. for the trillionth time, she wished she could speak without speaking.

i just get so scared, k went on. *you're the most beautiful thing in the world. men are afraid of that.*

love is a weak thing, limited by the physical. it can feel like there are more ways to hate than there are to love. sometimes k knows that this isn't the truth, but other times she is seduced by the fear that we'll never stop telling stories about how they hurt us, and that these stories are the only ones we have.

it has nothing to do with beauty, replied bea. she speaks more softly now, but her voice is still firm. *it's not my fault.*

i know, i know! k holds her closer. *i don't mean the way you look. i mean the way you are. it's why they want to hurt you.* she kisses bea's neck. *i want to kill all of them.*

me too, said bea.

i want to take care of you, said k. *please let me keep trying.*

this time, bea softened all the way.

GONE

hey, where are you?

it was Glory's name on bea's phone, but her voice is almost unrecognizable. she sounds (*afraid*) as if she is calling from the bottom of the ocean instead of a few train stops away.

well, says bea, glancing out the window again. the digital sign on the platform still says TRAIN DELAY. *i'm in Sacramento. i'm trying to go home.*

oh. Glory sounds both surprised and unhappy. *up north, right?*

yeah, says bea. she shifts in her seat. the first wave of sweat has dried, and now her clothes feel musty and stale. *why—*

can you come back? interrupts Glory. *i think it's important.*

come back? what is it? something must be very wrong. why else would Glory, who is her friend but only because she is k's friend, call her like this, call her at all?

there is another hesitation. this is not like Glory, to be so uncertain, so trepidatious, and the silence stretches out between them like the red line at the bottom of a video (*what happened to k?*), like the route back home, the train tracks laid down all the way to Oakland that run under bridges and tunnels and beside the highway, so perilously close to the waterline that bea can't understand why the ocean doesn't just swallow it up just because it can. fearful for k though she is, the effort of stopping herself from hanging up brings another wave of sweat across her body.

i'm not exactly sure, Glory admits. *but something's up with k. we need to find k.*

bea can feel the sweat bubbling to the top of her skin, trailing from beneath her hair. her heart is racing again. she feels as if she might drown in her own body. strange as it sounds in her ears, she clings to Glory's voice—*we need to find k*—and k's face wells up, her eyes and mouth swimming toward her through darkness. suddenly, k disappears, and for no reason she can understand, bea is back on the beach with Mai, fifteen again, feeling her arm against hers, a single gust of wind singing across their skin at the same time: a return to a happiness that existed just a few moments before her courage failed her.

hello? can you hear me?

bea only pauses for a moment longer. *i'll be there*, she says. she is still terrified, but her body feels less precarious. she realizes she can distinguish individual heartbeats again. after a few more minutes of talking, they hang up, plans made and action decided upon—just how bea likes it.

THE SORE

k doesn't remember putting on these pants this morning. it feels hard to get them off her body. when he offers to help her, she glares, but she lets him. he doesn't seem to notice that she's angry. he starts to remove his shirt. *don't do that*, k says. but he does it anyway, as if she hadn't spoken. her stomach still hurts, but this feels like a relief: she's still in her body, still in this place, still real (her binder warm and tight around her), even when he chooses not to hear her. she knows that now is not the time to lose contact with herself and lose control of the situation. her pants, underwear, and shoes are on the carpet, but she keeps her phone in her hand.

can you put that away? startled, k looks up again. he's nodding at her phone, his pink forehead catching the light. it's almost fifteen past 9 and Glory hasn't called.

a few years ago, on what she later described to Ken as a whim, but was actually a much less romantic impulse—she needed money—k put up an ad as a woman. she hadn't been getting a lot of action lately, and only the week before, someone had asked her to leave before he even let her inside his apartment.

you must of did something to your pictures, he said, examining her from the doorway. *i didn't know you were a female.*

it was in my ad, insisted k. *i told you when we were texting, too.* she didn't know why she bothered arguing. this deal was dead in the water. but it was just so unfair. and why? maybe he thought he'd try a little fish but then chickened out. maybe he was trying to haggle down her rate. maybe he was just a sadist. it didn't matter why. he just didn't want her.

other than wearing a dress that she'd borrowed from a friend, she went about her w4m date the same way she always did—no vetting, a little haggling, a text exchange before meeting him at his place. maybe her straightforwardness was why he'd seemed edgy from the moment he answered the door. right as she was beginning to wonder if he was just tweaking, he started to yell. she got away with one of her shoes, but not before he threatened to beat her tranny ass and almost tore off her dress. down the street, barefoot, trembling, almost weeping with gratitude that she still had her phone, she called a Lyft and collapsed on the curb. looking down into the gutter, tears bleeding down her face, she suddenly began to laugh. raucous as a crow, she roared into the space between her knees until she couldn't breathe. you couldn't make this shit up if you tried.

i like to keep it on me, says k. for a moment, he looks like he's going to argue, but then he doesn't. *just give me a sec.* she'll set it aside, but first she has to text bea (I love you) because she has to say something—even if it's not really anything. even if it's useless. even if it's the truth.

IN DREAMS

bea was on her second girlfriend the first time she had a nightmare that she was straight. and it was a nightmare; no dream could have spooked her so badly. always one to take stock in her dreams, bea was dismayed to rediscover the suspicion of her closeted years. the old fear—that she wasn't who she thought she was—had been inverted, repurposed, so that she could always mistrust herself, no matter what her body told her was true.

but as time went on and she got to know other queers, she learned that this kind of nightmare was no anomaly, that in fact there were many who had the same dream, one in which the life they lived, and the desires they felt, were false, and had been the entire time.

i used to get those a lot, said Ken. *they went away after i stopped talking to my parents.*

i've had a few, said Glory. *i don't know why, though. people saw me coming a mile away, ever since i was a kid.*

i don't remember my dreams, said k.

realness means something to queers because the world tells them that nothing that they do is real. even their love is a simulation, a sad mimesis of the basest kind. they are told that their essence is a performance (camp. trap. lie. phase.), no matter how technically perfect, no matter how convincing, and therefore a shadow, a shade, a sham. though queers insist that their loves and desires are as real as other people's (they do this by existing, by surviving, as well as by dying at the hands of straight people), it always seems that there is room for doubt. *maybe it will go away as i get older*, hoped bea, echoing prayers from years ago.

even with this fear, bea does not think of herself as a monster (*just a sore*), and she is thankful for this. she knows that not everyone is as lucky, as blessed.

THE BIG ONE

a fraction of a second after the blinds shatter, the lamp above their heads bursts against the wall. k's first thought: *bea.*

the shaking is unlike anything she's ever felt before, even the 7.0 of her childhood (awakening, her daddy's hair in her eyes, slung over his shoulder, *where is mommy*, outside and smoke and shouting, although she learned later there was no fire, at least not then, not until later (a neighbor left the stove on), *where is she*) she feels herself inside herself, her fingers searching for her clothes, her shoes, they're in her hands as she leaps up from the couch, backing toward the wall, eyes wide open, trying to turn herself away from inside herself, trying desperately to stay outside her body, searching for anything above her that might be heavy. behind the curtains, the blinds still rattle; metal screams in the kitchen.

what are you doing? somehow, his eyes are not afraid.

we have to get out! k says it with words, but she is not thinking of him when she says *we. (where is she? where is bea?)* the room is possessed. she can't find her underwear, so she pulls on her pants without them. somewhere to the side he is moving, touching his clothes, upending his drink with his foot. the darkness in the apartment spreads and grows and ignites as she stumbles into the kitchen *(where is she),* grabs for the doorknob, it doesn't turn (the time she and bea thought they were locked out of the car while they were camping and for a moment the pure and humming darkness of soft midnight woods had grown opaque, an enemy), but then the door gives, and k can run (his voice behind her, face pinker, socks on the carpet), across the hallway and to the staircase, landing against the wall, rebounding and running and tripping and then getting up to run again anywhere, because *(where is she)* she has to find her.

THE EARTHQUAKE ROOM

we went in that room, too, the one where the ground shakes and you can see the City burn up, said k.

oh my god, said Glory. *i've been in there. it's so corny. looks like they haven't touched it since 1997.*

i know, right? said k, laughing. *maybe that's what makes it creepy. i don't know, i think it weirded bea out.*

why? cuz it's gonna happen again?

well, yeah, said k. *i mean, it is scary* (QUAKEPREP WHIS-TLEBLOWER SENTENCED TO SIXTEEN YEARS). *i guess it bothered me a little, too.*

you know what they say, said Glory, *they say that the stuff that scares you the most has already happened to you.*

really? k didn't know they said this.

yep. i read that somewhere. i know it's that inspirational kind of crap, but i actually think about it a lot when i have anxiety. when i'm worrying about Arianna or my friends. or the cat.

·

well, i'm pretty sure i wasn't around a hundred years ago, said k. after they had left the museum, bea had told k she wanted to be alone and went home by herself. it was the only time k could remember bea not wanting her around.

bitch, don't be so literal.

well, the future isn't only stuff that's already happened, k went on. *that's why it's the future.*

the future is also what's happening right now.

k laughed. *what does that even mean?*

Glory sighed. *like when i think about the future, i think about people i care about. they're both the same thing.* she ran her fingers through her braids, examining the tail end of one through the glasses she only wore at home. *i am way too high right now.*

THE BIG ONE

k takes the stairs all the way down, once twisting her
ankle, but work doesn't exist right now, and even if it did,
it wouldn't matter because after this there won't be roads
to work on or food to deliver, won't be money to be made
or rent to pay, because the Big One is here (*where is bea*),
and she has to get outside, has to get to someone (*Glory*)
make sure everyone is safe but find bea (*my phone did i leave
it*—magically, it is in her hand), in potent shock that there
is still ground beneath her feet, the echoes of footsteps on
the stairwell popping up and clattering in her head (*is he
following*) one door slamming after another, so loud she can
only feel her phone moving in her hand (*Glory*), someone is
calling (*where is bea*), but before she answers, she has to open
the door, the very last door, heave it forward and step out
into the night. she looks down at her phone.

it's not Glory who's calling. it's bea.

THE BIG ONE

the door opens out into an alley, and k is around the corner
and back on the main street before she realizes it's perfect
outside.

the sidewalk is still flat on the ground. the dumpsters are
upright, and so is the woman—shopping cart packed to the
brim—picking through one of them. it is clear and cold
and dry, the only moisture collecting (jewelets in the night
lights, two houses high, on every corner) in clouds, like
insects, over the pristinely parked cars.

through the pain in her ankle, k feels her feet on solid,
motionless ground. the earthquake isn't here. the earthquake
that k willed into being, summoned like a witch, like one of
those brujas with black lipstick and seafoam tresses, altars of
stone and bone and imago (locket mothers; pocket Frida),
has never been.

but then she sees bea (*bea*), phone to her ear, her face glowing
behind honeyed hair, its expression something like panic. a
few feet away is Glory, standing on ginger tiptoes as she tries
to read the brass street number, her shadow a long, beautiful

spider on the wall of the building. k calls to them, almost dropping her phone as she pushes it back in her pocket, and they turn together (two heads of Cerberus, conjoined at the heart), both seeing k in the same instant. they run to her and throw their arms around her in a single movement.

Glory drives while bea sits with k in the back seat, her arm around her. the street is busy, because it's still early—barely 10—but as they get further from downtown, the lights start to disperse, the cars slow. on the surface of the Lake, the buildings bleed into shape, a cloud of blackness and shine that no ripple disturbs.

THE BIG ONE

they sit near the water because they don't know where else to go (*and you are a water sign, after all*, bea had once said. this had meant nothing to k). the air is cold, the sand grey with last night's rain.

k slept in her own bed through a storm she doesn't remember, one that, not unlike a dream, gathered and dispersed during the window of her unconsciousness. Glory offered to stay with her after they dropped bea off at her apartment, but k wanted to be alone. the words for gratitude were still too far away, but k hugged Glory first, and held on for a long time.

bea woke up much earlier than k did, but only because Glory was calling her.

sorry, said Glory. *wanted to check on you before i went to work.*

that's okay, said bea. *i was gonna call you, too. beat me to it.*

though bea thought they would, she and Glory did not talk about k. they did not talk about where they found k the night before, or betrayal, or the Woman in Black. in fewer than five minutes, they talked in simple terms about their feelings—no cause or effect, no agents or victims. it was not that those things didn't exist, or that they wouldn't talk about them soon (*we have always been afraid, but haven't we always loved, too?*), but right then was not the time.

when k woke up, the sky was clear and cold again, but out here by the water, where the howl of the waves drowns out even the birds, the sun is buried in clouds. it's not yet noon, but k is ready to go back to bed. she hopes bea will join her, but first she has to tell her everything.

when she's done—and it takes her a very long time—she waits for bea to speak, her terror that she never will mounting with each passing minute. in a panic, she blurts, *are you angry at me?*

this is not quite the question k wants to ask. what she really wants to know is: *can you ever forgive me?* she wants desperately to touch bea, to kiss her hands, to hold her close, but she knows she must wait, perhaps for a long time. perhaps forever.

as if to reassure k, bea nods her head, but she takes her time answering. her eyes scan the horizon, as if the words she's looking for are somewhere out there on the water. she wants to be very careful about what she says (*honesty*), because she knows how she feels, but not what she thinks—not just yet. finally, when k is almost convinced she'll never talk to her again, bea speaks.

i'm not sure, she says.

bea listens to the words now that they are outside of her body, and realizes, to her relief, that they are true. she loves k, and knows k loves her, but that's as much as she knows. (a revelation: love might not be enough) beyond that, anything is possible.

k feels her eyes filling with tears, and for a moment, she almost turns away from bea so that all she can see is the water, a giant slate on which an earthquake, even the Big One, would look like nothing at all. not that it would matter. the Big One—or whatever it was she summoned last night—has already happened, has already ended the world. it's too late to undo, too late to take back. she wants to make it up to bea, to make up for everything, but doesn't know if she can, or if it could ever be enough. *i don't know what's going to happen*, thinks k. tears spill over onto her cheeks. but she doesn't turn away, and bea sees this. the world may have ended, but this isn't the end.

beyond them both roars the ocean, an excess of sound. out there is space for everything: for the past and for the future, for the aperture of memory and for moving onward, for disaster and for healing. for seeing everything in existence and nothing but each other.

When [Saint Catherine's] confessor urged her to stop forcibly vomiting her food, she replied that such pain was penance for her sins and that she preferred to receive her punishment in this world rather than in the next.

[*The Culture of Pain* by David Morris]

"The Garden of Eden," pursued Mr. Emerson, still descending, "which you place in the past, is really yet to come. We shall enter it when we no longer despise our bodies."

[*A Room with a View* by E. M. Forster]

Appetite won't attach you to anything no matter how depleted you feel.

It's true.

[*Citizen: An American Lyric* by Claudia Rankine]

Thank you to TigerBee Press for taking a chance on me, and to Charlotte Shane for your brilliance, insight, and encouragement. Working with you is a dream come true, and I mean that in the corniest possible way.

Thank you to my dear friends for their support, excitement, and ministrations. What would I do without you?

Thank you, Kitty, for giving my story a face, and for so much more. Even though you've been there from the start, this is just the beginning for us.

And to Emily: Thank you for healing with me. I love you.

DAVEY DAVIS writes about culture, sexuality, technology, and genderqueer embodiment. Occasionally, they write fiction, too. They live with their partner and a cat in Berkeley, California. *the earthquake room* is their first book.